WICKED MAGIC

THE ROYALS: WITCH COURT BOOK 2

MEGAN MONTERO

LEO PRESS

To my Alexander, we are the best team ever and you are always my most favorite person in the whole world!
Xoxo-Mom

CHAPTER 1

ZINNIA

"We have to go after her." I wrapped my arms around Tucker's waist and buried my face in his chest. Hot tears streaked down my cheeks. Each one rolled off my chin and stained his ripped shirt. His body was unnaturally warm against mine. I leaned into him, finding comfort in his unbreakable embrace. The wind drifted over my face, taunting me with my mother's honeysuckle scent. *I lost her. Oh God, she's gone.*

The ache in my chest spread from my stomach all the way up to my throat. My breaths came in panicked puffs. I was getting no air and too much at the same time. My mother had just been kidnapped by the evilest being I'd ever seen in my life, and I could do nothing about it. Helpless didn't even begin to describe the hurricane of emotions I was feeling right now.

When I forced the barrier for Hexia to go back up, it expelled Alataris and all the Thralls he had under his control. He'd transformed innocent witches into Thralls, using them to threaten us all by controlling them with his black magic. I hated him for it. They were evil in its purest form and attacked the witches of Hexia mercilessly. It was all his fault.

I hadn't known or expected to expel them, but most of all, I hadn't thought he would grab my mother at the last second and take her with him. *This is all my fault.*

A soft sob broke past my lips. "We have to save her."

"We will, just not right now." Tucker wound his arms tighter across my shoulders, keeping me close to him.

Did he just kiss my hair?

I shoved at his chest. "What do you mean not right now?"

"We have to get back to the Academy." He clutched me harder to him while I thrashed against his towering body. I wanted to· be angry with him for holding me back, wanted to ignore the fact he had a point. But when I peered into his warm honey eyes, the fight left my body.

Tucker loosened his hold on me, then motioned to the pavilion where we just fought off Alataris' invasion. "Look around you, Zin. We aren't ready to go after him, and if we do now, we will all die. How would that help your mother? She needs us alive."

I balled my hands in fists and pushed at him with everything I had. This time, he dropped his arms completely and let me turn from him to face the direction Alataris had flown. My body thrummed with the magic I siphoned from the old stone protecting Hexia. It swirled around my fingers and arms in silvery streaming light. My magic, the magic I'd only learned about days ago. I didn't know how to control it, didn't know what I could do with it. All I knew was I had to learn, and I had to learn quick. "I can't think about that now."

He wrapped his hand in the crook of my arm, then spun me around to face him. Long dark strands of my hair fell into my face in messy waves. I tucked them behind my ears. It wouldn't help contain the windblown mess I knew my hair was.

Tuck leaned into me. "We have to go now. The whole crew needs medical attention and I don't want to draw it from the people of Hexia. Just look, Zinnia. Nova, Tabi, Serrina, and Adrienne barely survived this. And Grayson . . . Gray is lying in a tent recovering from the siren attack. We . . . are . . . not . . . ready. We need to go back."

When I looked around, I knew he was right. "I can't give up my mom, Tuck. I need her."

"I'm not saying we are going to give up on her. I'm saying we need to regroup, make a plan. Hell, give our crew a chance to heal their wounds." The muscle in his jaw flexed. "But we will get her back. I swear it."

Part of me wanted to turn and sprint headlong for my mom, but deep down I knew if we were going to help her, running to a fight I couldn't win would be worse. We'd already faced Alataris when we weren't ready and nearly lost everything. I wasn't prepared to risk my mother or the rest of them. "What if he hurts her?"

My mind reeled with all the ways he could torture her. I knew that cave-like cell well. Memories of the smell of decay, waste, and fear assailed me as if I were standing there this very moment. It was a jagged rocky cave with thick bars running from the ceiling down to the ground. While I was there I couldn't tell day from night. Time felt like it'd stopped. Now, my mother was trapped in that hellish place. When Alataris held me captive, he was on the verge of insanity. Now with her near, would he fall off the edge?

Tucker gazed off, seeming to think about his next words. "He won't hurt her."

"You don't know that. You weren't there, trapped on

that island with him. I was. I know it was only for a day. But it was long enough to know he's not just evil. He's crazed." I pressed my fingers to my mouth, trying to fight off the nausea rolling through me. My world was turned upside down in only a few days. I had yet to figure out my way and now this . . .

"You're right, I wasn't there, but there's one thing I know." He stood with his hands fisted at his sides, over six feet of towering menace.

At this time of night, he looked dangerous with the wicked phoenix tattoo he had running down the side of his neck. But I knew Tuck. He would never be a danger to me. Even after a battle he was still gorgeous in my eyes. His tousled hair was a mess of dark auburn falling just above his jawline. His shirt was torn all over, revealing the rippling muscles covering his torso.

I pressed my lips into a hard line and glanced at the destruction Alataris brought down on Hexia, the last free witch stronghold. "What's that?"

When he stepped in closer, his warm, woodsy scent washed over me. "Even he isn't capable of doing damage to your mom."

"You can't know that. There's no telling what he'll do next." As I looked at the shops around the pavilion, I couldn't pry my eyes away from the shattered glass, broken down doorways, and small fires everywhere.

Families huddled together under makeshift tents. They were covered in dirt, blood, and grime. The eerie silence was broken only by the cries of small children and moans of the injured. This was what I imagined a war zone would feel like. *He was here for less than an hour.* What would he do with my mom with an indefinite amount of time? Hexia was the last witch stronghold. Alataris had taken down the barrier within days. What did that mean for the rest of Evermore? What did that mean for her?

"I do know this: if your mom is Alataris' soul mate, she will be okay. Even he can't hurt his own soul mate." Tuck reached out and tugged me toward the end of the main road where a triage station was set up. "Come on, let's get back now."

My mother had used the dark sprawling mark around her wrist to distract Alataris long enough so I could save Hexia. She'd sacrificed herself for these people . . . *for me.* Tucker was right. We needed a plan to get her back. Which would take time and a detailed strategy. More than ever I needed to learn the full extent of my powers and how to use them. For now, I'd have to help get our crew ready to fight. I sucked in a deep breath, then swiped the tears off my cheeks. When I looked down at my hands, they were caked with dirt and streaked with tears. I could only imagine what my face looked like. White ash smudged my boots and the bottom of my leggings. "Let's go."

Tucker called out to Beckett and Brax. "You guys get Grayson. We have to go back to Evermore Academy."

Beckett didn't say a word. He simply turned and pushed Brax in the direction of where the medical tents were.

I spun around to find the other queens struggling free of the bindings that'd been wrapped around their wrists and ankles. Nova, Queen of Death, was the first to get to her feet. Her white-blond hair hung in a tangled, matted mess down the sides of her dirt-smudged face. As I approached them, she bent to help Serrina free herself from her bindings.

I dropped to my knees to pull the ropes from her legs. "Are you guys okay?"

Nova narrowed her eyes at me. "I got it, Zinnia."

I pulled my hands back like she'd burned me. "I was just trying to help."

"How did you know you could take all the magic from that stone? And how did you do it? Did Alataris tell you how?" Her accusing words were a slap to my face. In truth, I didn't know if I could do it, but something in me demanded that I do what I could to stop him. Nova pressed her lips into a thin line, then yanked the gag out of Serrina's mouth.

I sat back on my heels. "If I didn't try, we'd all be under his rule or worse, dead and drained of our magic. Is that what you wanted me to let happen?"

Serrina, Queen of Desires, pulled the ropes from around her ankles. When she looked up at me, for a moment I thought I saw fear. She was a goddess-looking girl with long flowing blond streaked hair, pouting red lips, and a punk-rock style that would have any boy begging at her feet. Yet as she looked at me with accusations in those emerald eyes, I felt like running the other way. How could she fear me?

She scrambled to her feet and grabbed my wrist so hard it pinched, then yanked me up. "Are you working with him? Tell me now."

Her power hit me so hard I stumbled back, gasping. It only took me a moment to adjust to it wrapping around my body. But as I stood there fighting not to let it in, I realized Serrina's powers didn't affect me. Unless I wanted them to. It was more of a nuisance than anything else. Was this something any Siphon Witch could do?

I fought to get my arm back, but she didn't let go. "What the hell, Serrina?"

"Are you with him?" She shook me so hard my hair fell into my eyes.

"Serrina, stop!" Tucker came up beside me and

grabbed her hand tight enough that it loosened her hold on me.

I yanked my wrist from her grip. Her nails scraped across my skin as I pulled free. "Are you insane? I just saved all your asses."

She crossed her arms over her chest and looked down her pert nose. "You can't blame me for thinking it. How did he know you'd be here when he captured you?"

I took a step back. "I don't know how! I was dragged out of a cave we all went into, remember?"

Tucker shoved between us. "Stop it, Serrina. He kidnapped her, and then she did everything in her power to get back here and save Hexia and us."

"Psh. What a power is it. When I heard of the siphon, I thought, great, we can finally unite. Not that my powers could be taken from me!" She pointed a finger toward me. "Just don't think you're draining my magic from me again."

Her words stung. I thought I'd finally found the world I belonged in. But standing here now I wasn't so sure. In all honesty, I didn't know who I was. A daughter? A friend? A soul mate? A Siphon Witch? Or even a Witch Queen? All I did know was that until I figured this out, I had to put on a brave face and show no weaknesses. Even if that weakness was them hurting my feelings. I lifted my hand up, letting the magic from the stone flow through my body and into my palm. I held it there, a silver sphere of power that stayed with me even after I made a new barrier. "Looks like I'm all filled up for now." I arched my eyebrow at her.

She glanced over her shoulder at Nova and Tabi. "Come on, let's go." She stormed off in the direction of the portal back to the Academy.

Tabitha, Queen of Elements, stopped for a moment, letting Serrina get farther away. The wind rustled her wild mane of curls, and dark smudges marred her light ebony skin as she sucked in a deep breath. She shrugged, and when she met my gaze with her vivid hazel eyes, I froze, waiting for her harsh words. "Don't take it too hard. I think she's just scared." She reached out and patted my arm. "She'll come around."

"Are you scared of me?" I didn't want them to be afraid of me. We were supposed to work together to take down Alataris. But if they didn't trust me, or worse, feared me, we would die like the other queens in the cycles before us. For centuries before this, the five witch casts would produce the five queens meant to take down Alataris' evil rule over the witch court. For centuries they'd failed and now it was time for a new cycle, my cycle. I might not know the world of Evermore yet, but I did know I would do anything to keep it safe.

"Honestly, yeah, sometimes I am." She gave me a half smile, then turned to follow Serrina.

Great, just great!

Nova stood with her arms wrapped around her midsection. She stared at the ground. "You know, Zin, I wish it hadn't happened like this. I am grateful for you coming in and saving us. But at the same time, I just wish your power wasn't so damn terrifying. I mean, you could turn us all to ash like you did to the old stone protecting Hexia."

The breath was sucked from my lungs. How could they think that about me? Hadn't I just won the day? Saved Hexia and all its people?

"Just because I turned the stone to ash doesn't mean I could do that to you or anyone else." I needed to get out of here. I needed to escape from their accusing looks. "I would *never* do anything like that."

I walked right past her, heading to no place in particular. All I knew was I had to get away from them . . . from here.

Tucker's footsteps thundered behind me, then suddenly, he was at my side. "Where are you going?"

"Away." My heart pounded in my ears, my hands shook with anger, and magic spilled out of me like I was a Disney character about to fairy godmother someone's ass.

"Away from where?" His warm, deep voice ran over my skin like velvet.

I froze and spun to face him. "Away from here." I couldn't stop my arms from flailing as I spoke. "I just saved all of you, in case you didn't notice. My mom was taken from me, and now all I'm getting in return is being treated like I ran over someone's dog."

"I'm not looking at you like that."

When I met his heated gaze, I knew he wasn't thinking I might turn him to ash too. His eyes were liquid honey, drawing me in.

I shook myself. "But everyone else is. It's not fair. I did something good here. I shouldn't be punished for it."

Tuck reached out and placed his hand on my upper arm and pulled me closer to him. The heat of his touch spread across my body. It was still night in Hexia. Fires were lit to keep the streets bright. In the glow of the dying firelight his skin appeared to be tan, and hints of auburn in his hair stood out to me. "They'll calm down."

He darted his tongue over his lips, wetting them. I wanted to go up on my tiptoes and take his mouth with mine. I wanted him to kiss me until I forgot the world around me, until I forgot about the queens, Alataris, and the fact my mother was gone. I drifted toward him, ready to press my mouth to his, ready to find the one place I might belong to in this moment.

"Tucker! Tucker, come quick." Niche's voice carried over to us.

He took a step back and shoved his hands down to his sides. When his eyes met mine, I knew he was leaning too close to me. One moment he looked shocked with his raised eyebrows and parted lips. In the next he smoothed his features, then faced Niche, who was running down the street toward us. Her fire engine red hair streamed out behind her. Her glasses bounced on her face with every step she took and her normally pristine white lab coat was now covered in dirt and blood.

He called out to her, "What's happened?"

She waved for us to come with her. "It's Grayson. He's . . . he's dying. The healers said he doesn't have much time left."

A nervous ball formed in my throat as Tucker wrapped his hand around mine and we both ran toward Grayson.

CHAPTER 2

TUCKER

At the end of the dirt road, five large tents stood with row after row of cots for the injured. I tried to keep my eyes forward and not stare at the carnage Alataris and his Thralls brought down upon Hexia. It was an impossible task. Everywhere I turned there were witches covered in blood, wrapped in bandages, or trying to help others. They lined the side of the street, waiting to get their turn to be healed. Large gashes marred their bodies from when Alataris brought the barrier down. The barrier around Hexia was like a glass wall, and when he siphoned the power out of it then dropped bombs, it rained shards on the people living here. Large chunks of the old barrier fell through buildings and made craters in the middle of the street. Even now, witches wound their way around them as they ran from place to place.

Witches rushed around the cots, binding wounds with thick white bandages and administering potions to heal those who were injured in the attack. The worst part wasn't the blood or gaping wounds. It was looking at the faces of the small children who sat next to their unconscious parents that killed me. They shouldn't have to endure this, not while I was a knight.

Zinnia pressed her hand to my forearm. "Tuck, we have to go to Grayson."

When did I stop moving? "Right, okay."

She nodded and followed behind Niche toward the portal. Niche called over her shoulder, "We have to get him to the school. They can do nothing for him here."

Zinnia quickened her pace. "He'll be okay. He has to be."

Everything about Zinnia was perfection, from her wild midnight hair down to her beat-up combat boots. It was more than the mark on my wrist, the soul mate mark I lied to her about, that drew me to her. If Niche ever found out Zinnia and I were bonded together, she'd have to send me away from her. I'd lose everything I'd worked all my life for. I'd trained to become a knight to save Evermore. Looking around Hexia, I knew they needed me now more than ever. But as much as Evermore needed me was as much as I needed to be near Zinnia.

Niche came to a shimmering doorway that looked like a blue pool standing on its side. She ran to stand beside it and waved us through. Zinnia hesitated just short of the portal, looking up at me with wide eyes.

I came up beside her. "What's wrong?"

She didn't look at me, just stared at the opening. "I've, um, never seen anyone pass away before."

I placed my hand on her shoulder. "And you won't today."

When she peeked up at me from under her thick dark eyelashes, her sapphire eyes sparkled with hope. "But Niche said—"

"That he was dying, not that he was dead." I reached forward and wrapped my hand around hers, then gave it a small squeeze. "So now we stop it."

Her eyes widened. "Stop death? I've heard of people get brought back from the brink of death all the time. But what can I do?"

"Yes, they do." I dropped her hand then waved her through and whispered, "And together we can do anything."

She stiffened beside me, seeming shocked by my words. A shaky smile played on her lips as she threw back her shoulders and stepped through.

I followed right behind her. I'd ventured into all different kinds of portals. Some were like stepping through a door and others were jarring, dizzying, and violent. This one was the latter. My body spun and twisted in all different directions, feeling like it was going to be pulled apart and put back together all at the same time. Just in front of me I could see Zinnia's arms and legs flailing. Her dark hair streamed out behind her and then she disappeared through a pinprick of light. Before it became too much, I dropped closer and closer to the exit. When I stepped through on the other side, I sucked in a shocked breath.

There in all his fallen glory stood Matteaus leaning up against the wall opposite me. His black wings were spread out against the stone wall, taking up at least fourteen feet, maybe more. He pressed a small cherry apple to his lips then with one bite he ate half of it. When he looked down his nose at me, a half smile tugged at his lips. "You look like crap."

"I feel like crap." I shrugged and moved to stand next to Zinnia, who had yet to speak.

"So, you guys got attacked by Alataris?" He said it so casually like he were asking if it was raining. Another bite. This time juice sprayed over his fingers.

"Yeah." I put my hands on my hips, waiting to see if we were done talking or not.

"Any injuries?" Again, he didn't move from where he leaned so relaxed, so casual.

"Grayson Shade is on his way back, so we can get him to the infirmary."

Matteaus shoved from the wall. "Grayson Shade, the vampire from the House of Shade?" He rolled his eyes. "You kids never make this easy on me, do ya?"

Zinnia's head snapped up. "What do you mean?"

"Never you mind that. Tuck, you make sure that baby vamp is okay. Otherwise you'll be coming with me to The House of Shade to talk to that *family*. And trust me, you do not want to do that."

"Why not?" I glanced over my shoulder at the portal. At any moment Beckett and Brax would come through with Grayson in tow.

"Would you want to deal with an elite force of vampires?" He sucked in a breath and shook his head. "Never mind, just see to it that he gets better."

As the leader of the knights and queens, it was my job to protect them all. I knew it. He knew it. But I guess he needed to hear the words out loud. "I'll see to it. Did the other queens make it back?"

Matteaus nodded. "Came in about ten minutes ago. I sent them to their dorms to rest."

Before I could say anything, Beckett walked from the portal. His arms were straight down at his sides and his hands were wrapped around two wooden handles. I spun and backed up against the stone wall. Beckett met my eye and shook his head. "It's not good."

As he kept moving forward, the gurney stretched on with a thick canvas wrapped around each of the wooden handles. Gray lay on top of it, unconscious and covered in injuries I couldn't wrap my mind around. Beckett kept walking until Brax came through holding the other side.

Behind Brax, Ashryn stumbled forward looking more exhausted than ever. Her sandy brown hair fell into her sweat-soaked face. Dark purple circles hung heavy below her forest green eyes. She had Adrienne's arm draped over her shoulder. With one hand she held on to that arm and wrapped her other arm around Adrienne's waist, practically carrying her.

A few days ago, Adrienne had tried to take the place of the fifth witch cast to help Zinnia during her ascension. It hadn't gone well, and she was still recovering. I rushed forward with my hands out about to take Adrienne's other arm when Ashryn stopped me. "She's just tired. I've got this. Help Gray."

Niche stomped through the portal. Her back was ramrod straight and her hair fanned out in all directions. She motioned for me to get moving. "Go. Just go."

The moment Zinnia got a glimpse of Gray, she

rushed to his side. Even I had to admit he looked awful. His normally pale skin held a sickly yellow color. Sweat soaked from his forehead into his hair, making his chocolate locks look matted, not his normal perfectly slicked-back style. Even the color had leeched from his lips completely. The bandages around his torso were soaked in crimson. The stain slowly spread out from his chest and down toward the gurney. The sheets beneath him were caked in dried blood, telling me this wasn't the first time he'd bled out.

With Zinnia on one side and me on the other, we hustled up the stairs from the basement of the Academy. The moment we were in the main corridor, the other students stopped in their tracks to watch our little injured parade. I waved my arm. "Move aside."

They parted and pressed themselves against both sides of the hallway. The hallways were dim in the early evening. In Hexia it'd be after midnight, but here it was only about six and the halls were packed.

Behind me I heard Matteaus snap at Niche. "Really, Niche? This vampire. Do you have any idea the wrath—"

"I'm well aware. Now if you'll excuse me, I have a student to save."

"Did you just dismiss me?" His voice was deep and astonished.

"Indeed." Her heels clicked on the cobblestone floor

with each step she took. But I no longer heard Matteaus'
thundering footfalls accompanying hers.

Overhead tiny pixies buzzed around. They were no
bigger than my thumb and looked completely unassum-
ing, cute even. With long white hair and childlike faces,
it was hard not to fall for them. But they had a nasty
tendency to bite. Even worse than that, they loved to
gossip and carry messages from student to student.
Even now, I heard each of them whispering about
Grayson Shade being on the verge of death.

I glanced over my shoulder and spotted Matteaus
swatting at them like gnats. "Not another bloody word
about this to anyone." His voice boomed down the hall.
"Gossip mongers!"

If I wasn't so worried about Gray, I would've
laughed. We turned down the hall and a white swinging
door came into view. Beckett planted his boot in the
middle of it and kicked it wide-open. On both sides of
the long rectangular room sat cots. The harsh overhead
lighting reflected off the white marble floors. At the
back of the room sat a single desk with an older man
behind it.

Round tortoiseshell glasses sat in the middle of his
hooknose. His mouth rounded into a shocked O when
he saw the group of us flooding into the room. He
jumped to his feet and came from around his desk to

meet us in the middle of the room. He motioned to the cot beside him. "Put him down here."

Beckett and Brax quickly laid him out on the white sheets. Then stepped away. I'd never seen them both so shaken. Becket held his hands folded in front of him. Brax, our gentle giant, shifted from one foot to the other, running his hand back and forth over his crew cut hair. Zinnia moved to stand beside the bed. Her eyes were round with shock and her pale skin was ghost-like.

Niche pushed to the front of us all and addressed the doctor. "I am Niche and this is—"

"I know who you are. Mentor to the witch court." His eyes ran over us. "I know who you all are."

"Very well." Niche shucked in a breath. "What we need—"

"I beg your pardon. What I need to treat this young vampire is for all of you to leave." He walked up next to Grayson and bent over him, then pressed his hand to Gray's forehead.

Niche glanced from the doctor at the rest of us and back again. "Everyone back to their dorms to rest. We will be in contact shortly."

I turned to walk out the door, but before I could make it even one step Niche called, "Not you, Tuck."

CHAPTER 3

TUCKER

The doctor straightened his stance. "Everyone, and I mean everyone."

"I appreciate the position you're in." Niche put her hands on her hips. "But get to work now, Doc. We are staying."

"Very well. And it's Doctor Thermomopolishe."

"Right, Doc it is." Niche hovered over his shoulder as he examined Grayson. Zinnia rose and walked to the other side of the room to give them privacy. I turned and followed her.

"Tuck, do you think . . ." Her voice grew thick, and she cleared her throat. "Do you think he'll be all right?"

I'd lied to her about so many things already, I didn't want to lie to her about this. "I honestly don't know."

The doctor lifted the bandages from Gray's torso and

reached inside, probing them. He lifted his other hand and snapped his fingers. Bottles, fresh bandages, and medical equipment floated across the room toward him. One by one he plucked the necessary equipment from the air as if his magic was a surgical nurse.

Gray's eyes shot wide-open and his whole body curled in on itself. A scream broke past his lips. The doctor shook his head, then dropped the bandages back into place and pulled Niche away into the far corner of the room. They whispered hurried words to one another.

Zinnia moved closer to me and placed her hand on my arm. Electricity shot through my body. I sucked in a deep breath, trying to calm my racing heart. Her sweet vanilla scent surrounded me. "What do you think they're saying?"

"I'm not sure." We'd both been through so much over the past few days and at this point I'd had enough. I stormed over to his bed and waved Niche forward. "Why is he still bleeding like that?"

The doctor stepped up beside her. His pink cheeks were oily, as if he'd been standing there all night sweating. The lights reflected off his bald head. "We can't stop the bleeding. This is some kind of old siren magic I haven't seen before. It's very dark. His skin won't mend together the way a vampire's should. According to

Niche, the healers at Hexia were trying for quite some time. They are among the best in the world."

Zinnia grabbed Grayson's hand and held it between hers. "Alataris." She growled his name like a curse.

I knew she and I were thinking the same thing. There was no way a siren on her own could do this to Gray, but with the help of Alataris' black magic, anything was possible. "It was him."

Zinnia squeezed his hand. "Gray, can you hear me?"

He peeked open his eyes. "Hello, love." His voice came out a weak, low whisper.

"How you holding up?" When she looked down at him, her eyes glistened with unshed tears.

"Oh, it's not all that bad really." This was the thickest I'd ever heard his British accent. A rattling cough broke past his lips. Drops of blood sprayed from his mouth. "Don't look at me like that. Been in worst spots than this. I'll be right as rain, just you see."

I motioned toward his bed. "He needs more blood. At the rate he's losing it, we've got to replenish him."

The doctor nodded. "Yes, Niche said they have been, but they were running out and he's still not healing. I have some here and I will give it to him. Whether or not it helps only time will tell."

Only time will tell? Not good enough. "Do we even have time?"

"That I can't tell you." He shifted from one foot to the other.

When I started this journey at the trials, I knew it was possible for one or all of us to die. But I hadn't suspected Gray to be the first one to go. Now, standing here before him as he knocked on death's door, I knew I couldn't lose one from my crew, not a single witch or knight. This cycle had to be different from all the others. For a millennium, five Witch Queens would rise from the five witch casts to fight against Alataris. The Knights of Evermore would join them in their battle. Each one was marked by fate. For a millennium, they'd lost, and each time the cycle would start again. Doomed to be repeated until one day Alataris' tyrannical rule came to an end. This time would be different.

I stepped forward to stand at the foot of his bed, determined to see him healed. I wouldn't lose Gray or anyone else. "Then use magic." I jabbed my finger in his direction. "Heal him!"

The doctor wavered from head to toe. His deep purple coat rippled with each of his movements. "They have been using magic. B-but it's not strong enough to heal wounds of this nature."

I gritted my teeth. "Then get me another healer who can."

The doctor swallowed and took a step back. His eyes

bulged out of his head. "Mr. Brand, this is a school. You can't just order the staff around like this."

"Watch me." I crossed my arms over my chest.

A soft chuckle drifted up from Grayson. "Don't bark at him, Tuck. You're scaring the poor bloke."

Zinnia arched an eyebrow at me, then gave me a half smile. "I think he already has."

I cleared my throat and glanced toward the doctor. "Sorry, Doc."

He adjusted his glasses. "It's not a problem."

I crossed my arms over my chest and leaned back on my heels. "There has to be something we can do. He's a leech, for God's sake. Give him a ton of blood and he should heal up."

"Oh, I think the tweetie bird would miss me if I bit it." Gray's eyes drifted closed for a long moment before he opened them again and gave me a wilted smile.

"We have tried. Nothing is strong enough to fight off this magic." The doctor pulled a folded cloth from inside his robes and dabbed it across Grayson's sweat-soaked forehead.

"Nothing but me," Zinnia whispered.

I froze on the spot. "What'd you say?"

"He should drink my blood. I have the most magic, and it could fight against Alataris' hold." She held her wrist out over Grayson's mouth. "Drink me."

27

I threw my hands out. "Hey, whoa, wait just a sec. You don't know if that's going to help him. The magic from the old siphon stone could very well be too powerful."

Grayson barely held his hand up. "Wait a minute. I'm not *biting* her wrist."

"You're right." Zinnia threw her hair over her shoulder, exposing her neck. "It'll be faster this way."

They were talking as if I hadn't spoken at all. I wanted Grayson healed as soon as possible but not at the cost of Zinnia. It didn't matter that I didn't want to see his fangs in her . . . *not one bit . . . not at all . . . I'm good with it . . . kind of . . .*

Niche stepped in closer to Gray. "It just might work." She waved the doctor forward. "What do you think?"

"I think it is possible and certainly couldn't hurt." The doctor motioned over the side of Zinnia's neck, and the dirt and grime lifted away from her skin. *He's cleaning her neck for him to bite her?* My stomach rolled. This wasn't happening.

I nearly leapt forward and shoved Zinnia away from him. I didn't want another guy sinking anything into her . . . let alone his fangs. Yet there she sat with her long, graceful neck exposed for the taking. I could feel Niche's eyes on me, watching my every reaction. I was torn between wanting to save my friend and keeping my soul mate safe. But with Niche studying me, I had to lock myself down.

I stood still as stone, trying to think of a way to make this easier. "What if you did it by IV?"

"The problem with IV is we might lose her magic or the potency of her blood." The doctor shook his head. "No, it has to be like this."

Grayson wrinkled his nose. "From the flesh?"

No, not her flesh! I wanted to stop him. My mind raced with any other way of making this happen. I pressed my lips into a thin line.

Niche shrugged. "Or you could die. Your choice . . ."

"That's cold." Grayson's face fell into a mask of pain. He pressed his hand over his midsection, then winced and groaned.

Zinnia leaned over Gray. "Can you sit up?"

He sucked in panting breaths and shook his head. "I don't think so."

"Okay." Zinnia pressed her lips together and nodded. "I can do this."

No, you can't. My pulse raced in my veins as Zinnia leaned her body over his. I knew Grayson would die without her blood. It was our only chance. But the jealousy I was experiencing right now felt like I would die if she did. The inside of my palms burned. I knew without looking that my flames were answering to my emotions.

She tilted her head to the side. Her cheek was so close to his. Could he smell her sweet vanilla scent, feel the heat of her body pressing into his? Did her soft hair tickle his skin the way it tickled mine the first time she kissed me?

His lips pulled back from his teeth, and his fangs popped out, elongating to razor-sharp points. He sucked in a deep breath, and his chocolate gaze met mine a moment before he struck like a snake. Then his eyes slid shut as he swallowed down his first mouthful. Zinnia gasped. Her body shot tight with tension, and her back was ramrod straight. His lips were pressed to her neck like a kiss. Watching him *feed* from her was like watching an intimate act between two people. I'd expected it to be messy with streaming blood everywhere, but this . . . it was gentle and almost sweet. I wanted to look away, to get out of there as soon as I could. But with Niche standing there watching my every move, I had to keep it together. *Good thing I'm trained for this. Wait, did she just . . . sigh?* If Gray lived through this, I was going to kill him.

When he wrapped his arm around the small of her back, I nearly summoned my sword to cut his arm off. The color returned to his cheeks in a rush, and he slowly sat up, bringing Zinnia with him. They faced each other on the bed, with her legs dangling over the side and her chest pressed to his. *Where the hell is a clock when you need one?* It felt like they'd been at this for years.

Just as I was about to break them up, Niche stepped forward. "I think that's enough, Mr. Shade."

Thank God. I didn't know how much more I could take of this. Grayson tilted his head back, pulling his lips away from her delicate skin. Two small puncture wounds stuck out to me like spotlights. Before she could say anything, he leaned back in and ran his tongue over the two marks.

I clamped my fist at my side. "Isn't that enough?"

Grayson pulled his head back and smiled at me. His eyes were hooded with desire or satisfaction—I didn't know. He swiped his thumb over his bottom lip. "If I don't seal the wound with my saliva, she'll walk around bleeding all day long." He gave *my* Zinnia a long side-ways glance. "Why, my dear Zinnia, I do believe I'm a bit . . . *magic happy.*"

I couldn't take it anymore. Watching them together like this was something even I couldn't do. I'd suffered years of combat training, mental exhaustion, nearly been swallowed by a monster and dying. This would go down as one of the worst things I'd have to endure.

I gritted my teeth together. "Better?"

Zinnia pressed her hand to her neck, gently probing the puncture wounds with the tips of her fingers. When she turned to look at me over her shoulder, I couldn't meet her eyes just yet. I knew I was being unreasonable. I knew she'd just saved his life. I knew she had to do it . . . I knew I was being an ass. But right now, I didn't trust myself not to show her exactly how I felt.

Grayson stepped out of the bed and pulled those blood-soaked bandages away from his torso. His skin was already beginning to knit together, leaving behind tiny pink puckered scars. "Much better."

"Good." I turned and walked out of the room.

CHAPTER 4

ZINNIA

"Tucker, wait."

I turned on the cot to face the door Tucker had just gone through. I knew if I went after him now Niche would know something was happening between us, but the truth was I didn't even know what was between us.

Beside me, Grayson ran his fingers over the fading pink scars on his chest and stomach. "I've got to tell you, don't let any other vamp know about your super blood because they'll be after you right off. I mean, you're delicious."

Heat rushed to my cheeks, and I suddenly felt the need to cover my neck. I pulled my hair down around my shoulders. "Um, thanks?"

He darted from one end of the clinic to the other. All I could see was a blur.

The doctor's eyes followed his movements nervously, and he took a step back toward his desk. "I-I'll just be on my way."

Grayson leapt on top of the cot and held his arms over his head. "Whoa, I feel amazing."

"Mr. Shade, that's quite enough. Lie back down in that bed. We don't know that you're completely fine just yet." Niche pointed to the cot, then narrowed her eyes at him over the top of her glasses.

"I think I'm just going to go." I rose up from the cot and scurried from the room out into the chaotic hallway. Dizziness assailed me, and I teetered on my feet. I held my hands out, trying to stop the world from spinning. Nausea rolled in my stomach. Black dots swarmed my vision. I stumbled, and the stone floor rushed toward my face so quickly I didn't have time to put my hands out. Before my cheek smacked into it, two strong hands swept under my arms and brought me back to my feet.

A warm, woodsy scent invaded my nose, and I sucked in a deep breath, trying to get the world to right itself.

His rumbling voice lulled me into a sense of calm. "Zinnia, are you all right?"

"I think so." *I'm not all right.* I was seeing three separate Tuckers, which wouldn't be such a bad thing if I didn't feel like throwing up on two of them. He slowly came into focus, and I realized I was still standing. Well, kind of standing. My knees were buckled beneath me, and my fingers were digging into his biceps, holding on for dear life. In that moment, I was grateful for his strong hands keeping me up.

"You don't look okay." When he turned his head to the side, strands of his deep auburn hair fell into his honey eyes. If I wasn't so busy using him to stand, I'd reach up and brush them back from his face.

I forced my legs to straighten, and I loosened my grip on his arms. "Is this better?"

"You're pale."

"And you're hot." I slammed my hand over my mouth. *Did I really just say that out loud?* Heat flooded my cheeks. "What I meant to say was you're not hot. I mean, you are. But you're not?"

A chuckle rumbled deep in his chest and sent shivers down my spine. "So, I'm not?"

"You are." What was happening to me? It was like my brain just stopped working.

"I am?" He raised his eyebrows.

"Yes, no. I mean, damn. Can we just forget the last

five minutes?" I swayed on my feet. "I think I need to sit down."

"I think you need some sugar." The muscle in his jaw ticked. "You gave too much blood to Gray."

His voice was sharper than his normal smooth timbre. I almost flinched back from him. "Are you angry at me?"

At this time in the early evening students were finished with their classes and just hanging out around the hallways. Some of them slowed as they passed us, staring at Tuck and looking at me like I might sneak into their rooms in the middle of the night to write words in blood on their walls. *I'm not that kind of witch, guys!* A pixie floated down and landed on Tuck's shoulder. She sat perched there with her legs crossed at the ankles as she braided her long white hair. Then she rose up on her tiptoes and danced along his shoulder up to his ear. At first I thought she was whispering into it, then I realized she was about to bite him. I lunged forward, trying to swat her away. Before I could, Tucker reached up, caught her in his hand, then tossed her away.

"No." He couldn't meet my eye. Instead, he glanced over my shoulder, looking anywhere else but at my face.

I rose up on my tiptoes and forced him to meet my gaze. "Hey, what's going on with you?"

"Did you like it?" The words tumbled out of his mouth. He pressed his lips together. "Wait, don't answer that."

"Did I like getting bitten by a vampire?" Was he serious? How could I like having someone's teeth in my neck?

He sighed. "Just wondering what your thoughts were on getting dental."

I rubbed at the two small puncture wounds on my neck. They ached and throbbed. "Can't say it's something I'd like to repeat again. Wait, did you just say *getting dental?*"

He shrugged. "I've heard it can be . . . pleasurable."

Other students openly gawked at us as they walked in all different directions, going to dining hall, or the library, or even to after school clubs. All the things I'd like to be doing at this exact moment, yet I was tasked with fighting an evil king and trying to save the world. Not to mention having one of the most awkward conversations with a guy I was crushing on hardcore.

I glanced around. "Why are they all staring at us?"

"Par for the course of being the witch court. We've got a lot of work to do." Tucker dropped his hold on me, then turned and walked away.

I stood frozen, wondering what had just gone so wrong. "Tucker?"

His shoulders stiffened, yet he didn't turn back. I stumbled forward, following in his wake. All around, students moved out of his path as he stormed down the hall. Somehow, I managed to catch up to him.

Before he could get away, I wrapped my hand around his shoulder and pulled him around to face me. "What is wrong with you?"

"Nothing." He crossed his arms over his chest.

Deep down I felt he was lying. Over the past few days, the more I was around Tucker the more I could feel his emotions out. I wasn't sure if it was because of my growing magic or something else. But it was unnerving. "Don't lie to me."

"I'm not."

"Sure, you're not." I wasn't going to stand here and play *guess my emotions* today with him. Enough was enough. I'd been bruised, battered and bitten all within twenty-four hours. I backed up a few steps. "You know what? I don't need this right now."

I'd just saved all of Hexia and Grayson, yet everyone was looking at me like I'd betrayed them, or I was dangerous.

Tucker followed closely behind me. "Zin."

No, I wasn't turning around. I was done with this day, done with all of them. "Leave me alone."

"I can't." He sighed. "I can't leave you alone."

I whirled on him. "And why is that? Is it because you're my knight, or is it something else?"

I was so tired of secrets. For sixteen years my mother kept from me who I was. Now standing before him I wanted to know what he was hiding.

He glanced down at my wrist and then quickly away. "I just want to make sure you're safe."

"Mission accomplished." I started walking back toward the portal that was connected to Evermore Academy.

"Zin, wait."

"Wait for what? For you to tell me how I'm going to find my mom, or beat Alataris, or how to use my magic without nearly killing everyone? Or even better yet, wait for you to tell me what this mark around my wrist means?" Only hours ago, my mother flashed her wrist at Alataris, calling it her soul mate mark, distracting him long enough for me to destroy one stone and make another. Did that mean the mark on my wrist was a soul mate mark too? If so, then who was my match?

"I can't tell you." He looked down at the ground and shook his head.

"Yeah, that's what I thought." I started walking again.

He leapt into my path, stopping me from moving forward. "But I want to."

"Ugh." I threw my arms up. "Then why don't you?"

"It's complicated."

I jammed my finger in his face. "That is not an answer."

His shoulders sagged forward. "I want to tell you, but I can't."

"Why not?" I put my hands on my hips.

"I can't tell you that either." He kicked at a rock with the toe of his boot.

"Bye, Tucker." It was time to end the day. Exhaustion filled my body. I'd lost a large amount of blood. I couldn't remember the last time I ate anything, and now this. No, I was so over it all.

"Zi—"

I shoved through the first classroom door I saw. I'd expected to walk into an empty room filled with chairs. What I got was something completely different. I stood on the edge of a sandy white beach with the sun beating down on me, warming my skin. *What the heck? Did I just portal again?*

Tucker shoved in behind me. "We shouldn't be in here. Let's go."

I knew I was angry at him, but at the same time I didn't understand how one minute I was in the school and the next I was standing on a beach. Every portal I'd ever traveled through was turbulent, but this had been so easy. I held my hands out to my sides, feeling the warm breeze brush against me and ruffle my hair. "How is this possible?"

Tucker came up beside me. "Evermore Academy has thousands of students who need classes on multiple subjects. To find that kind of space in New York City would be near impossible. So the school has a space charm on it. The base of the school stays the same with the courtyard, dorm rooms, and four towers for classes. But whenever they need more, it's always here, ever changing Evermore." He wrapped his hand around my arm and tugged me back to the door. "Now come on, let's go."

I pulled my arm free. "No. I think I'll stay here for a while."

"Look around you, there is a reason other students aren't in here hanging out on the beach."

Teal waves rolled against the shore. I sucked in a deep breath of that salty air. For the first time since I'd gotten to the Academy, I felt relaxed. I shrugged. "I'm staying."

Tuck opened his mouth to argue with me, but the sound of paws stampeding toward the beach stopped him. I turned to look back at the palm tree covered island. The trees were shaking and there was a clear path where they were splitting and falling to the ground. The path kept getting closer and closer.

"What is that?"

"I don't know. But I don't want to stay to find out." Tucker grabbed my arm and started dragging me forward.

I planted my feet. There was something inside me telling me I had to see what creature was coming at us. The last set of trees parted and a wolf—no, not a wolf, a beautiful creature the size of a small car popped its head through. It had the body of a wolf, with dark black fur that had vivid blue markings. When it stepped through completely, I noted how its fur shimmered in the sunlight. When I got a full look at it, I was shocked to find it had at least nine tails. Each one pitch-black and tipped with vivid blue. The creature dug its front paws into the sand and launched itself at us.

"Zin, now." Tucker threw me over his shoulder and ran straight for the door.

"Put me down. I have to touch it." I reached my hand out to the creature and it was getting so close. Its nose was only a foot away when Tuck leapt through the door and slammed it shut behind him. I kicked my legs. "Why'd you do that?"

He dropped me onto my feet. "Because that's a Kumiho."

"A what?" I peered at the door, yearning to go back.

Tuck hunched over and sucked in deep breaths. "A

Kumiho. It's a creature that was trapped in a painting until some idiot painted all nine of its tails on. Once it got out it attacked humans, trying to make itself human. Luckily, the Fallen were able to get it bound to its animal form. But, Zinnia, that thing is a killer."

"Then why keep it in a school?" My eyes shot wide as I eyed the door anew. I could hear it scratching at the other side like a puppy wanting to get in.

Tuck shrugged. "The study of mythological beasts class."

Even hearing what Tuck just said I still felt a bone-deep pull to be in that room with the Kumiho. I knew he wouldn't let me go back in there, but my instincts were telling me I had to. The first chance I got I was going in that room.

"I'm serious, Zin. The answer is no." He crossed his arms over his chest.

My anger rose to a boiling point. Instead of yelling, I sucked in a deep breath. "I guess it's a good thing you're not the boss of me."

Bright red flooded his face. "Seriously?"

We stood staring at each other. The energy bounced between us and I couldn't tell if it was anger or something deeper. My heart raced, and I stepped in closer to him. For a moment I didn't know if I wanted to kiss him or kick him. His honey eyes turned molten as he leaned in closer. I wanted him closer.

"Tucker and Zinnia." Niche marched up to the two of us. Instantly, I felt she was about to yell at us. I took a small step back. Though Niche was smaller than me by only an inch, her fire engine red hair, big glasses, and white lab coat gave an air of authority I couldn't ignore. She held her head high and shoulders squared.

I snapped to attention. "Yes?"

She came to stand between us. "Let's keep our focus. We need it now more than ever."

What did that mean? Did she think there was something between us or that my mind wasn't where it needed to be? Like on Tucker and all the reasons why he wouldn't let himself get closer to me even though he so clearly wanted to.

Niche pushed her glass up her small nose. "Tomorrow I want Zinnia to start training with her powers, and let's find her a weapon she can be comfortable with."

I inwardly sighed with relief. This wasn't about my personal life or me sneaking into classrooms holding dangerous creatures. This was about the role I was born into. Funny how I'd rather face that than the messy pieces I was turning into over *him*.

Tucker nodded. "I'll see to it."

"Great, we all good here." I needed to get away from him. I needed a moment to breathe. But most of all, I just needed a damn moment, period. "'Cause I'm gonna go back to my room now."

I took a step away from them, but then I felt his hand on my shoulder for just a brief second. "I'll walk you back."

I glanced at him. "That won't be necessary. I think we're done here."

CHAPTER 5

ZINNIA

I hadn't slept all night. Tuck was in the dorm room next to mine and I could hear every move he made through the night. He tossed around just as much as I did, and each time he did his bed creaked. Then my eyes would shoot wide-open and I'd lie there listening for his next move. Yesterday had been too much of an emotional rollercoaster and I needed the sleep. But I barely got more than a few hours. I just wanted to focus on my classes and wait for the next opportunity to face Alataris. This morning I got up early and was just about ready to sneak out of my room. I held my books close to my chest and slowly closed my door behind me.

"Ms. Heart!"

I jumped at the unexpected sound of my name. My

arms flew up and I dropped all my books onto the floor. Each one that hit the ground sounded like a bomb going off. Professor Davis stood in front of me and placed her hand over mine. "Oh my dear, I'm so sorry to startle you."

She was a shorter, rotund woman with a jolly aura that I found pleasant to be around. Every time I saw her, she wore traditional robes in deep purples and pinks. All of them had detailed embroidery and swayed along with every waddling step she took. Her frizzy salt and pepper hair always stood on end as if she stuck her finger in an electrical socket.

"It's okay." I bent down and began collecting my books as quickly as I could. I hadn't heard his door open or close. He had to be in his room still. When I reached for my book of potions, a large hand was already there picking it up. I glanced up to meet honey-colored eyes. His warm, woodsy scent enveloped me. I sucked in a deep breath and tried my best to calm my racing heart.

He handed my book to me. "Morning."

I grabbed it and placed on top of the pile I was carrying. "Hi."

As I stood, Professor Davis smiled at the two of us. "So sorry to surprise you, dear. But I had to see you straight away before you left for your classes."

"Is everything okay?" I lumbered under the weight of my book and struggled to hold them all up. Why I thought bringing every single book for every single class I took was a good idea was beyond me. *Oh right, trying to avoid Tuck.*

"Let me." Tucker reached over and took half the books from my hands. His face was smooth and calm, but deep down I felt him simmering under the surface. It'd been there since last night. I wasn't sure the tension between us was going to calm down anytime soon.

"Such a gentleman." Professor Davis gave him a wide smile. Her round face reminded me of a smiling jack-o-lantern with bright red cheeks. "Everything is just fine, dear. I came to give you your new schedule."

I reached out and took the paper she handed to me. "Why do I have a new schedule? The old one was just fine."

Professor Davis rocked back and forth on her heels. Her puffy salt and pepper hair stuck out from under the little cap on top of her head. "Well, in light of the events of the past few days, headmaster Matteaus thought it best we amend your schedule. To better fit your particular skill level."

Great, just great! I've been here for a couple days and my schedule is already being changed. "Oh."

"Don't you worry. I'll be seeing you very soon." She winked at me then walked by the both of us.

I didn't want to look up at him, but even if I didn't, I felt his presence like a second skin. I looked down at the ground and shuffled from one foot to the other. Tucker reached over and grabbed the paper from my hand. "Let's see what we have, shall we?"

"Just a sec." I turned back to my room, opened the door, and dropped half of my books down, then emptied out some more from my backpack. When I walked back into the hall, Tuck stood there holding some of my books and looking over my schedule. Girls in the school stopped in their tracks to openly stare at him. Yet he stood there looking oblivious to it all. Even the school pixies collided with each other in midair because they were watching him.

When I walked over to him, I noticed more than one girl giving me dirty looks. I ran my fingers through my hair, trying to tame the wild waves. "Okay, I'm ready." I held my hands out for the rest of my books.

"Ready to stop avoiding me?"

Caught red-handed. Damn.

He gave them to me along with my schedule.

I pulled my backpack around to my front and shoved my books in and peered down at my new schedule, trying not to look at him. "Who, me? I wasn't avoiding you."

"Oh no? I'll pretend tiptoeing out of your door was to avoid the pixies." He pushed the sleeves of his black shirt up to his elbows, then brushed the strands of hair from his forehead. I couldn't take my eyes off his tan skin and the muscles beneath.

"Okay, maybe I was avoiding you." I hiked my bag higher up on my shoulder and began strolling down the hallway.

Tuck moved to my side, silently walking with me. "Why?"

Because I can't stop thinking about you and you are forbidden fruit. I shrugged. "No reason."

"Uh-huh."

Awkward silence fell between us. The tension was palpable. "My next class says it's on the third floor. But it just says 3232R?"

"Remember that room you stepped into last night?"

"Yes?" *How could I forget the Kumiho and the sparkling beach?* We walked out of one hallway and across the courtyard. Goose bumps broke out over my skin and my breaths puffed out in white smoke. Drops of water misted across my fingers as we passed by the fountain and I wiped them on my black leggings.

"It's ever changing Evermore. You go to the third

floor, second door then in that hallway, then the thirty-second door on the right. That should take you to your class. Hopefully that'll put you in the right class."

"Hopefully?" I glanced up at him as we walked under an archway and into another hall. Though it was only late September, the air was cooling rapidly, and I felt the chill deep in my bones. I wrapped my arms around myself.

"Don't worry." His lips pulled up in a half smile.

"Yeah, I think I'm the type who worries about stuff." How was I going to get used to this world and used to the way I felt when I was around him? That mark on my wrist flashed into my mind. I shook it away. "Look, just don't let me get lost."

I followed him through another door and up a spiraling set of stairs. The same stairs I'd seen a boy fly off of only days ago.

Tucker peered down at me. "I'd never let you get lost."

I brushed a lock of my hair behind my ear and looked around, wondering if anyone else heard him the way I did. Was I reading too much into the things he said? I sucked in a deep breath and held it. Once we reached the second door on the floor, I hesitated. "What if I'm bad at this?"

He brushed his finger over the end of a lock of my

hair. "Zin, you were born to do this. How could it go wrong?"

RIGHT, how could it go wrong? I ducked behind a desk along with the other students in my class. Another chair flew over my head, then smacked into the wall and I sank down lower. The girl next to me shook her head then rolled her eyes. "You would think a queen would know better."

"I couldn't help it."

The girl sneered. "You took down the barrier to Hexia, but you mess up a simple summoning spell? Oh, come on."

I wanted to reach out and smack her, but I was trapped where I sat. The sound of shattering glass and broken tables filled the classroom. "That was all instincts. This is different. And for your information I did summon something."

The girl had dingy blond hair and a pinched in face. She puckered her lips like she tasted something sour. "Well, go help then. Use your *instincts.*" She snickered at me.

The truth was I didn't know what to do. Professor

Davis stood at the front of the class, facing off against my mistake. "Zinnia, could you come out here, please?"

Though she spoke calmly, I could hear the nervous timbre to her voice. I knew it was dangerous, but I had no other choice. "Okay."

I moved out from behind the desk and stepped to the side.

Professor Davis didn't look up. She kept her eyes on the ground. "Just for reference, the next time I tell you to summon an animal, I was thinking a cat or a bird, maybe a dog. A mouse would be a great idea. But not this."

I nodded and kept my eyes on the floor as well. "I didn't mean to. It's just what came into my head."

"Well, now we have to send it back, okay?"

I nodded. "Okay." I glanced up at her.

Professor Davis grabbed my hand. "Don't look up."

"I won't, I won't." I shook my head. "Tell me what you want me to do."

"Let's just be calm and . . ." I didn't mean to tune her out, but I felt the same pull I felt last night. I had to look up. I had to see. I had to know. Little by little I raised my gaze. I started at the creature's oversized midnight paws, then up its long, muscular legs. Its broad chest slashes of striking blue markings over it. The blue marks stood out even more up against its black fur. The creature had the body and head of a wolf, but came up to my shoulder.

I took a step forward. "Kumi."

She snapped to attention. A desk hung from her mouth like a chew toy.

I pointed to the ground. "Drop it."

Her mouth fell open and the desk clattered to the floor. All nine of her tails swished together, wagging back and forth. The sound of them smacking into the walls thundered around the room. I took another step closer to her. "Good girl, now let's just calm down. Can you lie down?"

Her answer brushed against my mind, not so much as words but more like suggestions. And right now she was suggesting I stop talking to her like a baby. I held my hand out. "Fine, then lie down and stop making a fuss."

Kumi dropped to the ground and huffed at me. Professor Davis moved next to me and wrapped her hand around my elbow. "Zinnia, can you, can you hear her?"

I shrugged. "Kind of." When everyone gave me wide-eyed looks, I hesitated. "Can't you all hear her too?"

They shook their heads back and forth. *Awesome. Yet another thing that isn't normal about me.* Professor Davis took a step toward Kumi, but the giant wolf bared her teeth and growled. The professor skittered back behind me. I wasn't just going to stand here and let her bully everyone. I strolled up to her and pointed my finger in her face. "You stop that now."

Professor Davis stepped in closer to me. "Can you hear all animals?"

I shook my head, thinking back to the box of puppies I'd seen in Hexia. "No, it's just her."

"Hmmm, interesting," the professor mumbled behind me.

Kumi closed her lips, then whined at me. I shook my head. "If you want to go out and about, you need to have some manners, you know? No one is going to trust you if you go around growling and biting at people."

The class gaped at me, but Professor Davis spoke so calmly. "Now, let's reverse the spell, shall we?"

I nodded. "Yes." I didn't want to cause any more trouble.

"Very good. Now remember you have to open up your inner magic and say the words with conviction. Use every bit of your power behind each syllable."

I sucked in a deep breath and thought about my words carefully, knowing they had to make sense and flow together like a song or epic rhyme. I held my hands up and closed my eyes. When I called upon my power, it was there deep inside of me, waiting to be used. "From whence you came you must return. To the sandy shores where you will not burn. Take thee now from my sight back to the place filled with Evermore's light."

I pictured the sandy beach I'd found her in last night, pictured the door I'd walked through. A second before she disappeared, I felt the sadness she felt, the loneliness she'd been living with all this time. I whispered, "I'll come visit. Promise." Then she was gone back to where she came from.

Professor Davis clapped her hands together and spun in a twirl around. "That was marvelous, absolutely marvelous."

The girl in the back of the room climbed to her feet. "How can that be marvelous? She summoned a demon dog. It destroyed the class and nearly killed us all."

"Now, Patty, let's not exaggerate. The Kumiho didn't attack anyone. It simply wanted to play. And as for the room, well, I've seen much worse."

As I peered around the class, I noticed its *playtime* was more out of control than any pet I'd ever seen. Desks were scattered around the room, each one toppled on its side. Paper litter the floor and the students all looked like they'd been through a tornado. Professor Davis walked over to one of the chairs and picked it up. "But you see, Zinnia has shown that she can indeed master spell casting."

I pressed my hand to my chest. "Me? After I destroyed the classroom?"

"Technically you didn't do it. Kumiho did." She shrugged. "I believe, Ms. Heart, that you will do very well with your spell casting. You just have to embrace it."

Embrace it. Riiiiggghhhhtttt. "I think I'll just read up on it a bit more before I try again." *Like a lot more.*

CHAPTER 6

C ool fall air whipped through the courtyard of Evermore Academy, sending my hair flying around my face. I huddled deeper in my leather coat, pulling the collar up against the frigid wind. How could the temperature drop so much in the single day I was away? As I walked by the large fountain, I saw a thin layer of ice forming on the top of the water. *Really?*

Two stories of the rectangular Academy surrounded the courtyard. Each one was open to the outside and sectioned off by archways. It barely broke the chill falling over the city. Off of the courtyard there were multiple hallways leading out toward other buildings around campus. To my right was a hallway that led to the witches' tower, where I would study the craft. To my left was a hall that led to the training center. Normal high schools would have a gym, but definitely no weapons. The Academy specialized in preparing the youth of Evermore for anything and everything. From what I'd seen firsthand, the supernatural world of Evermore was a beautiful, dangerous place to live in. So, there were lots and lots of weapons. None of which I knew how to use.

A sharp gust cut through the courtyard, forcing me to clutch my books tighter to my chest and curl my shoulders under. I was suddenly thrilled with my decision to wear a scarf with this outfit. At least I'd wear it until I got to the gym assigned to Niche's queens and knights. Yesterday I was told to report for training. Today I was ready in my black leggings and off-the-shoulder sweatshirt. Even though I'd never trained for anything a day in my life, this was what I thought a warrior wore when they trained, but what did I know? I'd never held a knife, sword, or crossbow.

Tabitha came up beside me and started walking toward the training room with me. We were complete opposites. Where I wore all black and an olive-green scarf, Tabi was covered in bright colors from head to toe. With a thick cowl neck sweater that hung down to the middle of her thighs and covered her matching pink leggings, she looked like a flower. Her hair was pulled high on her head in a little puff ball of curls.

Two curly midnight tendrils hung down on either side of her face. If it snowed, I had no doubt her bright pink outfit would reflect off the white surrounding her.

She gave me a half smile. "Hey."

"Hi." After the way the other queens looked and spoke to me yesterday, I didn't know how to act around them, including Tabi. Seems I couldn't do anything right lately. I pushed a lock of my hair behind my ear and kept looking forward. Before I came to Evermore, I never really fit in with anyone at the many schools I'd been shuffled around to, but when I came here, I'd hoped I would. Now walking in silence with Tabi, it made me miss the best friend I left behind. Elle. She'd never be afraid of me, no matter how unpredictable my power was. It only made me more determined to learn to control it.

"Listen, Zin. Yesterday was a rough day for us all. And I might've said some things I didn't mean. I'm sorry. It was just scary being taken so easily. You know? We're supposed to be these super powerful witches." She hiked her backpack up on her shoulder as we left the court-yard and headed down the hall.

"Yeah, I get it." I didn't want to hold a grudge against any of them. But if we were supposed to work as a team to defeat Alataris, we had to be comfortable with each other. And right now, I wasn't feeling it. "When he took me, I didn't expect it either."

Tabi nodded. "I'm sorry."

"It's okay." *Is it?* My feelings still stung after they'd turned their backs on me.

"Causing more trouble, Zinnia? Surprise, surprise." Patty from my class marched by with a few of the other girls trailing behind her.

I glared at her and muttered, "Surprise, surprise. Patty Pinch Face."

Tabi's chest rumbled with laughter. "What did you do to Patty Bowerguard?"

"Ugh, I had a little trouble in spell casting class and I'm pretty sure she won't ever let me live it down."

Tabi leaned in close to me as we walked. "And she's going to keep giving you a hard time. Her family is one of the oldest in the witch world. The fact you are a queen and she isn't bothers the crap out of her. I do one of two things when it comes to old Patty Pinch Face."

"What's that?" I met her excited hazel eyes.

"Ignore her or dish it right back. I have to say dishing it back is much more satisfying."

I couldn't help but laugh. "I'd think so."

As we approached the double doors leading to the gym, I saw Serrina and Nova standing just outside of them with their backs to us. They leaned into each other, whispering and laughing together. I wanted to leave them to what they were doing and wait just a little farther down the hall to give them space.

Tabitha seemed to pick up on this and lightly pinched the sleeve of my shirt between her fingers then gave it a slight tug. "Come on."

"I think I'm just going to wait here." I leaned back against the wall.

"It's going to be fine. Come on." She pulled me again.

I have to try, right? Right. I followed behind her.

A wide smile spread across Tabi's face as she came up next to Nova and Serrina. "What are we looking at?"

Serrina startled and waved her hand at us to be quiet. "Shh, they don't know we're here yet."

I went up on my tiptoes and peeked over Nova's shoulder. In the gym, the knights were in full-on training mode. Tucker stood in the middle of the room wearing nothing but a baggy pair of black sweatpants and combat boots. Sweat poured down his body, giving his pale skin a glowing shine. In one hand, he held his flaming sword low and out to the side. With the other, he pointed with his finger at Beckett and Grayson. His wicked phoenix tattoo was on full display from just under his jaw and down the right side of his neck. The tail feathers curled just at the top of his right peck. His muscles moved and flexed with each of his movements, and those black sweatpants hung so low on his hip it was . . . *delicious.* My heart sped up. *Damn.*

He motioned toward Beckett. "Stairs now."

Beckett hunched over and sucked deep panting breaths. His surfer blond hair was slicked back against his head with sweat. "Come on, we've been at this for hours."

"And you'll keep going until it's right. Stairs now." He held his sword up, and I swear I could feel the power he used to control those flames. They crackled down the white metal, sending off bright red sparks.

Beckett leaned back on his heels and began tossing blue spheres of magic into the air. They lined up one right after the other.

Tucker nodded. "Good. Gray, go."

"Yes, boss." Grayson ran at the stairs at full speed. His arms blurred into his body until he was just a streak of white moving around the room. He leapt up, taking the sphere steps one at a time. When he reached the middle, twenty feet in the air, his toe caught on one of them and he tumbled forward. His arms pinwheeled wildly as he headed to the ground face-first. It was like a train wreck I couldn't turn away from.

Ashryn, the noble elf, pulled an arrow from the holster on her back, then drew it on her bow faster than I thought possible. She let it fire right at Grayson. The arrow went straight through the hip of his pants, jerking him back and stopping him from falling. Instead, the arrow shot straight into the wall behind Gray, pinning him there by his pants.

He hung limply for a moment before waving toward Ashryn. "Thanks for that, love."

I'd only seen her shoot on a few occasions, but each time I did, I found myself more and more impressed with her. She tossed her sandy brown hair over her shoulder, wild braids mixed in with her long strands. The tips of her tiny pointed ears peeked out from between them.

She sauntered up beside Tucker. "This move needs work."

As one of the knights of Evermore, she'd be training with Tuck and the others. At times when she looked at me with those hunter green eyes, I felt she was looking right through me and seeing secrets no one else could. There was something different about the elves. They were calm and somber, almost to the point of being utterly cold. Ashryn was no different. In the short time I'd known her, she was unflappable. She was all long lean lines, and her movements were fluid, like a dancer. Standing at just five and a half feet tall, she was a couple inches taller than me but completely dwarfed by Tucker's height.

Tucker sighed. "Yes, it does. Do it again."

Serrina whispered to us, "Isn't he the hottest one? I mean, the line to get Tuckered is long enough. Imagine if he walked around school like that."

Yeah, imagine that. I bit the inside of my cheek to stop from laying claim on him in front of everyone.

Nova shook her head. "No way, it's Beckett. He's the hotter one, for sure."

I don't see it. Beckett was beautiful in a surfer guy kind of way. With his tan skin, light blond hair, and ocean blue eyes, he was good-looking for sure. But there was a dark primal undercurrent in Tucker that called to me, attracted me, like a moth to his flames.

I leaned in. "Nah, it's Tucker all the way."

As if he heard me, his head snapped up and his heated gaze locked onto mine. Heat pooled in my belly. *Does he know I'm talking about him?* His lips pulled up into a half smirk. He called out to us. "Ah, glad you're all here. Let's go."

Grayson yanked the arrow from his pants and soundlessly landed on his feet. "Yes, glad you're here, now your torture can start and ours can stop."

Niche strolled in from a door on the other end of the room. "Tucker Brand was trained by Balthazar Black-wing, one of the greatest warriors ever. I recommend you listen to him, Mr. Shade."

Grayson threw his hands up. "Is it me or do you always turn up at the wrong moment?"

"It's you." She shrugged and continued past him. She glanced down at her clipboard then back up at where we stood. "Ladies, right on time. Very nice."

Niche pressed her pen to the board and drew a small check mark. "Tuck, I assume you have this well in hand. I need to get back to planning." Without another word, she turned and went back into the door she'd come out of only a moment ago.

Beckett leaned over and rested his hands on his knees. "I tell ya, Gray, she has some kind of locator spell on you. Every time you're about to do or say something stupid she's there."

"I know, right?" Gray walked up to stand on the other side of Tucker. "It's all the bloody time."

Tucker clapped him on the shoulder. "Just remember you're the one who said you do something stupid all the time."

Then he stepped away and motioned toward us. "Let's go, ladies. Time to train." He waved us into the room.

I sucked in a deep breath and followed Serrina and Nova over to the side of the gym where they dropped all their stuff. The moment I put my books down, I felt something akin to panic in the pit of my stomach, yet my heart wasn't racing. I was calm. *Tucker.* I spun on my heels, then threw my arms out, shoving Nova and Serrina off to the sides and out of the way of his swinging sword. The flames weren't there. Had they been, he might've caught one of us.

I leaned back, and the tip of the razor-sharp edge missed my face by mere inches. "What the hell, Tuck?"

He pointed his sword at Serrina, then Nova, and then at me. "Never let your guard down, not even for a minute." He took a few steps back. "Not bad, Zinnia."

Not bad? I extended my hand out to Serrina to help her up off the ground. "Sorry for knocking you over. Gut reaction."

She took my hand and let me lift her to her feet. She brushed her hands off on her shirt then down her sides. "I guess if we were in a fight, that would've saved my life."

I shrugged. "Maybe."

She crossed her arms over her chest. "You're like a super witch or something."

"Or something," I mumbled. I'd never had a day of hand-to-hand training in my life, yet I felt Tucker coming. Why? Was it some kind of witchy sense, or was it because since I laid eyes on him I felt more and more connected to him? Either way it didn't matter. I had to learn, and I had to do it quick. For my mother, for Evermore, and for myself.

"Well, whatever it is, I'm glad you're on our side." She gave me a half-smile.

"Are you?" I gave her a sideways look. "Because yesterday you all but accused me of being on Alataris' side."

"Look, I was just terrified in the moment, and I took it out on you. Honestly, if you hadn't done what you did, we would've probably died." She pressed her hand lightly to my elbow. "Thanks."

What the hell was happening around here? Dealing with all their emotions was going to give me whiplash. "You're welcome?"

"I'm glad Tuck talked to me about it this morning. We can't have a rift between us all." Her bright red lips pulled up into a perfect model smile.

"Wait a second. Tuck talked to you about it?" Why would he do that for me?

She shrugged. "Yeah, he wants us all to get along. I mean, we do have a world to save, so I get it." She turned away and headed to the corner of the room where Brax stood waiting with two wooden swords. When she got closer to him, he tossed one up in the air, which she caught instantly.

I am not that good.

Nova got up off the floor and pulled her long white hair high into a messy bun on the top of her head. "Thanks."

Nova turned toward the wall and pulled down two small wooden daggers. When she spun them in each of her hands, I felt I was nowhere near their level in anything. Maybe my fight with Alataris was a fluke, and winning was pure luck. I took a step back, ready to turn for the door and find a self-defense class 101 to start with. Maybe even kickboxing for starters.

Tucker motioned for me to join him. "Zin, you're over here."

I balled my hands into fists at my sides and pressed my nails into my palms. *I can do this. I can do this. I can do this.* Of course, Tuck was at the center of the gym where everyone could see. Why couldn't we be in a corner like Tabi? She looked totally comfortable in her private section, wielding a golden whip like it was child's play. Adrienne stood beside her with her own silvery whip, showing Tabi new moves.

I pointed toward a darker spot in the gym. "Sure you wouldn't be more comfortable over there?"

Tuck plucked his shirt from the floor and ran it over his face and chest, wiping away the sweat. *Yeah, that's not distracting at all.* He shook his head. "No, here's good."

"Great, so, um, what do you want to do first? Swords? Knives? Machine guns? Throwing stars?"

He chuckled and shook his head. "You think you're ready for me?"

Definitely not. "Bring it on."

"Be careful what you wish for."

CHAPTER 7

Funny to think yesterday I was nearly dead and today I was standing back in the training room about to take on the most powerful witch in a generation. My only saving grace was she still didn't know it. I owed her more than I could say. Her blood saved my life, and now it was time for me to teach her to save her own. But as I approached her with my throwing stars at the ready, a tide of emotions overcame me. Emotions that weren't my own. I'd been a vampire all my life, and with that came the knowledge of knowing when my internal radar was completely jacked up. Right now, I was rolling like the ocean.

What is wrong with me? As I approached Zinnia, she bounced on the balls of her feet nervously. In turn, I was nervous. *Bloody hell.* I never got nervous during training.

Zinnia turned to me with wide eyes. "Are you going to throw those at me?"

"Maybe." I chuckled.

Her face paled, and she shook her head. "Nope, I'm not some kind of super vampire ninja."

I stopped in my tracks. My heart was racing uncontrollably. I tried to ignore it. "I said I'd throw them at you, not that I would hit you with them, love."

I pinched the side of the star and tossed it at her. It circled around her body like a boomerang and came right back to me. The gleaming silver metal reflected the harsh overhead lights of the gym as I caught it. "See? Mystically reinforced to come back on my command."

A small smirk tugged at her bow-shaped lips. "Cool?"

"It is indeed." My heart started to slow back down to its normal speed. Was it a side effect of Zinnia's magic in my blood? Was my body not handling it?

Then Tucker strode up to Zinnia, holding out a sword in one hand and a dagger in the other. He presented them to her. "Which one?"

She bit her bottom lip, and again my hands started to shake with nerves. When she reached out to grab the sword from him, her hands tremored slightly. *Oh crap!* Was I feeling her emotions because of a blood tie? When she glanced up and her eyes met Tucker's, I felt an instant zing between them. That was when I knew there was indeed a blood tie. I shouldn't have been able to feel her emotions or anything else. *Damn, what am I going to do?* Back home in the House of Shade, we did not drink from the flesh under any circumstance. Yet yesterday, I broke that rule, and now I was feeling thrown off and out of sorts.

The moment she lifted the sword up, she nearly toppled over. She stumbled forward, and the blade lodged into the mat at her feet. Pink tinged her cheeks, and I felt the rush of embarrassment she now felt.

I walked up beside her. "Perhaps something lighter, mate."

Tucker reached down for the hilt of the sword at the same time Zinnia did. When their hands brushed, my heart started to go wild once more. *Bloody hell no.* Ugh, she wanted him like nothing I'd ever felt before. I staggered back as the breath left my lips in a rush. *Wait a second. Just wait a sodding minute.* There was something else in there, another hint of someone else. Someone who wasn't Zinnia or me. All these different emotions were almost too much, but there was something inside of me that liked having this insider knowledge. Now to figure out who the other one was…

"I got it." Tucker wrapped his hand around the hilt of the sword and effortlessly slid it from the mat on the ground.

Zinnia's cheeks turned an even darker shade of pink. "It was bigger than I expected."

I scoffed. "That's what she said."

Zinnia jabbed her elbow into my arm. "You're so gross."

"I quite like the way I am." I winked at her.

"I like the way you are too." When a light giggle escaped her lips, I was hit with a wave of jealousy so strong I felt the need to duck away, as if a fist would come flying at my face at any moment.

Tucker shoved the knife in my direction. "Here, give it a try with this."

Ah, we have a ringer. As he stomped away from me, the pieces started to come together. I glanced from Tuck at Zinnia and back again. *Ah, Grayson Shade, you are brilliant sometimes.*

A plan began to form in my mind, and the vampire in me couldn't help but want to meddle in the affairs of others . . . *Uncle Titus would be proud.*

CHAPTER 8

ZINNIA

"Zinnia, sweet, why don't you try this instead?" Grayson handed me the dagger.

"I have a thought." Tucker strolled back up to us. He quickly plucked the dagger from my hand and tossed it away. He held his hand out to me with his palm up. A ball of white light gathered at the center of his hand, and a set of two small half-moon looking blades sat beautifully in his grip. The handle was perfectly straight and wrapped with a black leather. The blade itself connected from one end of the handle to the other. The silver metal glinted in the light. I grabbed them out of his hand and held them at my sides. They were light and well-balanced, with a small half-moon carved into the side that mimicked the witch queen mark on my shoulder perfectly. When I turned them over, there was a small flame carved into the other side.

"How do you do that?" I held the blades out in front of me. They felt like natural extensions of my arms, weightless like all I would have to do was swing my hand out and I'd connect with my target.

"Do what?" Tucker watched as I twisted my wrists around, moving the blades.

Grayson leaned his arm on my shoulder. "You know, that little bit of making weapons appear in your hand. How do you do that?"

Tucker narrowed his eyes at Grayson. "It's old shifter magic. Not sure a little vamp like yourself could master it."

"Right, I'm sure if the pretty bird can do it then a brilliant vampire can." He met Tucker's gaze and wagged his eyebrows.

"Can I do it?" If I could summon weapons the way Tuck did, I might stand a chance in combat after all.

He shrugged. "Anything is possible."

Grayson held his throwing star up. "You sure you wouldn't like one of these? Small but effective."

Tucker chuckled. "Is that what you tell the ladies?" Then he held his own sword up. "Or you could use something like this if you don't like the blades."

"As fun as this whole *my weapon is bigger than your weapon* thing is, I can't take your blades from you." I held them out to Tucker. "You need them."

He shook his head. "Keep them."

"I can't, Tuck. They're too beautiful." I jiggled them in my hands. They were perfect, but I couldn't stand the thought of taking them.

He glanced at Grayson, then leaned in closer to me. "I made them for you."

"Jeez, mate. What ever happened to flowers and chocolates? Here, lady, have a knife . . . to kill things with. Nothing says *hey, I like you* like a weapon of destruction." Grayson threw his head back and chuckled.

I shoved his arm off my shoulder then narrowed my eyes at him. When I turned back to face Tucker, he shuffled from one foot to the other, his eyes downcast. "I love them. Thank you."

"You're welcome. And they're enchanted like Gray's ninja stars. If you throw them, they'll come back to you." When he gave me that half-smile, the butterflies in my stomach flipped around.

"Wow, really?" I stepped away from him, then wound up and let the blade go as if I were throwing a baseball. It spun in graceful circles like a Frisbee across the gym.

When it circled back around, it cut through three separate ropes hanging from the ceiling. One after the other, punching bags dropped to the ground. Each one hit the floor with a resounding *thud*. Everyone stopped what they were doing to openly stare at the mess. The spinning blades didn't stop there. On their way back to me, they ricocheted off the cement walls, sending tiny sparks into the air. The sparks landed in a pile of discarded towels, setting them on fire. Smoke rose from the pile, and little flames licked up the side of the wall.

As the blades got closer to me, I knew I couldn't do this. Images of them lodged into my palm assailed me.

Tucker seemed to know exactly what I was thinking. "Just open your hand and call for them with your mind."

I closed my eyes and turned my head away. In my mind, I imagined them landing in my palm hilt-first. "Crap, crap, crap."

The buttery leather of the hilts slammed into my hands, and my shoulders jerked. Before I fell over, I took a step back, righting myself. "Well, I'll be damned."

"Yeah, not bad, not bad at all. Only a small fire and mass destruction." Gray poked my side. "That'll do."

I pressed my lips into a thin line. The noise around the gym fell silent until Serrina hunched over and started laughing. "Well done, Zin. Not quite as bad as my first training session. But close. Hey, Nova, remember when you raised all those Reanimants, and they chased us around here for an hour?"

Grayson shivered at my side. "I hate those zombie-looking things."

I shook my head. "I don't even want to know. Do I?"

They all shook their heads at the same time. Gray leaned into me. "Listen, Zin, we've got to have a bit of a chat later, all right?"

"I think anything you have to say to her you can say in front of me." Tucker crossed his arms over his bare chest.

Before I could answer either one of them, a rush of footsteps sounded down the hallway. The walls vibrated, and a loud roar cracked the windows at the top of the gym. I looked up at the ceiling. "What was that?"

Tucker rushed toward the double doors leading to the hall. He reached his arm out and wrapped his hand in the shirt of the first boy he saw. He pulled him through the doors and back into the gym. "Start talking now."

The boy had to be all of fifteen years old. His face was dusted with big round freckles, and his eyes were so wide I saw more whites than I did the brown. "D-d-d-dragon."

Tucker dropped his hold on his shirt. "A dragon is attacking the school?"

The boy nodded. "Alataris."

I didn't hesitate. I ran headlong toward the dragon and Alataris.

CHAPTER 9

ZINNIA

I pumped my arms, running toward the courtyard. My heart raced in my chest, and a sheen of cold sweat broke out over my body. I didn't know what I was going to do once I got there. All I knew was I had to stop him from hurting my school. It was a strange thing being terrified and yet still sprinting toward exactly what you were afraid of. Behind me, heavy footsteps thundered along. Without looking over my shoulder, I knew the others were following me. It was our duty to protect Evermore from Alataris, and right now, he was crossing a line. Evermore Academy was ruled by the Fallen. Every supernatural knew it. So Alataris was either completely crazy or was here for a specific reason.

Once I hit the courtyard, I skidded to a stop. The

fountain in the center of the Academy was frozen solid. The ice looked like it formed within seconds. Spurts of frozen water drifted out from the top tier in jagged spikes. In the second tier, streams of ice waterfalls connected to the bottom tier of the fountain, giving it the effect of a miniature ice-skating rink. Six inches of snow covered the ground. Flakes clung to my hair, clothes, and eyelashes. Cool air seeped through my sweatshirt and leggings. A chill ran up my spine, sending goose bumps skittering all over my body.

Students huddled under the archways, while others ran for cover. I marched out into the middle of it all and gazed up into the sky. At first, all I saw were thick puffy gray clouds, the same I would see on any winter day. Yet it was late September. A freak blizzard was completely out of place in New York City.

Outside, the noise from the city was muted by the falling snow. I tilted my head from side to side, waiting for Alataris to walk out to face me in the courtyard with his dragon. I expected it to be something out of a movie, where the dragon spoke of riches and wanted to be king under a mountain.

What I got was something entirely different. Through the thick clouds came the deafening roar. I hunched over and covered my ears until it stopped. Then it slid out from between the clouds. Wings the size of houses flapped quickly, propelling the dragon high above the school, circling around. It was huge, with bright white scales, which were the shape of seashells. Each scale had a blue rim around it. The wings were smooth like a bat's and were also white with blue mixed in. *The movies had it wrong.*

A black harness was fastened around its back. The belts strapped around it pinched into its scales. Before I had to wonder where Alataris was, the dragon banked to the side and there stood Alataris, riding on its back. A bridle just like the one used for horses trailed back from its mouth. With one hand, Alataris held the bridle, and with the other, he snapped a whip at the back of the dragon. Each time the barbed end of the leather whip smacked into its back, the dragon roared louder.

I lifted my hand with my blade still tightly clutched in it. I screamed, "Alataris!"

His head snapped to the side. His dark soulless eyes met mine, and he actually smiled. On the back of the dragon, he looked like a long stick figure. His arms and legs were gangly and spider-like. His thick black hair peeked out from under a bright red snow hat. The rest of him was covered in a one-piece brown snowsuit, like he'd stolen it from a construction worker. He inclined his head, giving me a small bow, then yanked back on the reins of the dragon. Its head thrashed from side to side as streams of snow and ice poured from its mouth. Like an avalanche, it dropped from the sky straight toward me.

My body was knocked sideways, and I found myself ass deep in a pile of snow with Tucker pinned on top of me. "What the hell, Tuck?"

He hesitated with his body hovering just over mine. His face was so close our noses nearly touched. "I'd prefer if you weren't buried alive."

Just as the words left his mouth, a mound of snow dropped down in the place I'd just stood. When I gazed up into his honey eyes, I sucked in a breath. "Thanks."

"No problem."

"Um, Tuck?" I looked around at the others staring at the two of us.

"Yeah?"

"You want to let me up?"

He scrambled back onto his knees and cursed under his breath. "Sorry." As he stood, he pulled me up next to him.

"You were right. I'd rather not be buried alive." I brushed the snow from the back of my pants.

I gazed up at Alataris and gritted my teeth. "Missed me!"

"Badass." Tucker chuckled.

Alataris didn't think so. He pulled the reins tighter,

and again the dragon thrashed at the hold and blew more ice and snow. The snow behind me crunched with heavy footfalls.

When I turned to look over my shoulder, I stumbled back. "Matteaus."

Matteaus was rumored to be the oldest living supernatural in Evermore. He and the other Fallen ruled us all with an iron fist. His hulking black wings seemed even darker among the white landscape. I was used to Tucker's six-foot-three-inch stature, but when Matteaus strolled out next to him, he made Tucker look small. Matteaus' arms were the size of my head, and when he wore only a black tank top and baggy jeans, the sheer mass of him was on full display. There were locks of his hair falling into his eyes in a display of browns, blonds, and some light reds.

He pushed his hair out of his face and then came to stand next to me. "Why am I not surprised to see the two of you out here?"

Tucker gave him a sideways glance. "We didn't plan to drop a foot of snow on the school."

"Indeed, you didn't." Matteaus cupped his hands around his mouth and yelled up at Alataris. "Albee! Don't make me come up there!"

He scolded Alataris as though he were a small child rather than an evil king trying to take over all of Evermore. When Alataris didn't turn to move on, Matteaus slowly extended his wings out to his sides. Old power crackled in the air around me. I could feel it weighing down in the courtyard. Alataris' eyes widened, and before I knew it, he turned the dragon away from the school.

I stepped forward. "You're just going to let him get away?"

Matteaus shrugged. "Can't interfere."

"Why not?" I wanted him to go after Alataris and take him down here and now, to end this.

"For reasons I don't have to explain to you. You want to deal with him, go after him now." Matteaus turned on his heels and strolled away.

Ugh! A little help wouldn't hurt! Anger burned through my body. I didn't know what to do or how to even use my powers fully. But my instincts roared at me not to let him get away. I turned away from Matteaus and shoved Tucker in the chest. "Phoenix, now!"

He raised his eyebrows for only a second before leaping up into the air. His body twisted and turned in a ball of burning fire. Yellow and orange light burst from him, lighting up the white snow like a summer day. Two huge wings flared out from the ball of fire, and suddenly, there was a phoenix half the size of Alataris' dragon flying around the courtyard. He spun around my body, then shot up into the air. When he tilted his head to the side, his message was clear as day to me. *You coming?* He swooped downward, gliding over the ground like a pelican over water.

I tossed my blades down into the snow, then ran at him as fast as I could and leapt forward, landing square on his back. "Let's do this."

CHAPTER 10

I straddled Tucker's back as he flapped his wings harder, trying to catch up to Alataris and his dragon. I pressed my body lower to him and wrapped my hand around the base of his wings. Soft crimson feathers tickled my skin, and I squeezed him with my thighs, the way I did whenever I rode on a horse. "Faster, Tuck."

Flames burst from his tail, and we propelled forward like a rocket. Freezing wind whipped across my face, biting at my cheeks. Up ahead, I spotted the dragon's long tail with large white spikes at the end of it. It was like flying through a tube. All around us were large puffy gray clouds that blocked everything else from sight. Alataris stood on the beast's back, whipping it into a frenzy. I pointed at him. "Up ahead."

I didn't know what I was going to do or how we were going to stop him. All I knew was he had my mother held captive somewhere and he'd terrorized Evermore for long enough. Perhaps we wouldn't have to have an outright battle. Maybe we could do something else to stop him. "Tuck, what if we knock him off?"

He cawed a loud agreement, but it also drew Alataris' attention.

He looked over his shoulder, giving me a snarling smile. "Your luck has run out!"

Tuck dove forward and wrapped his thick black talons around the dragon's tail. When he dove straight down, I felt myself lift off his back and go completely weightless before I pulled myself back down. The dragon teetered to the side, flipping Alataris over. For a second the beast's underbelly was exposed. There in the center of its chest, where a scale seemed to be missing, was an orange glowing molten spot. Could it be that easy? A spot where all you had to do was hit it at the right angle and the dragon would die? Before I could get a closer look, the dragon twisted away and raked its claws at Tuck. We barrel rolled to the side, dodging the swiping claws. I hung on for dear life as my legs dangled away from his phoenix form. I clutched the base of his wings harder. In Tuck's human form, it'd be where his arms met his shoulders. When he righted us, Tuck screeched a warning, then sucked in a breath. His entire body puffed up, and I could feel it heating beneath me. He parted his beak and spat fire toward the dragon's neck. It reared back and roared in pain as flames licked at its white scales. A moment later, ice spewed from its mouth in an arch of white puffs. Tiny sharp shards rained down on us. They slashed at my sweatshirt and pants. I squealed and covered my head with one arm while holding on with the other.

Alataris hunched over and cackled from his perch. Then he snapped his wrist, and the whip coiled up into a perfect circle, which he then slid into a holster at his hip. A ball of red swirling magic gathered in the palm of his hand, then it began to spark the way a firecracker did right before it exploded. He tossed it at me like a baseball, firing it right at my head. I tilted to the side, forcing Tucker to dive away to avoid the ball. It exploded behind us. A loud boom echoed, and bright fire lit up the sky. The bright colors reflected off the gray clouds like it was the Fourth of July. Tuck extended his talons once more and raked them down the dragon's back thigh. Though he didn't break the scales, the dragon cried out once more. Its deafening roar pierced my ears. Another ball of magic came at us.

This time I plucked it from the air and held it for my own. "Tuck, you ever play chicken?"

Again, that loud cawing came from his chest, and he flapped his wings faster to get ahead of Alataris and his killer dragon. When he spun around to face them, Alataris had stopped the dragon. They floated in the air, holding the same position. Its large wings beat up and down.

Alataris' lip pulled up in a snide snicker. "You can't win here. Your bird friend is no match for my dragon."

I tossed the glowing ball up in the air and caught it. "Maybe not." I shrugged. "But it's worth a try."

I was ready to charge them head-on, to take on Alataris and let Tuck have at the dragon. I was about to tell Tuck about the soft spot I saw on its chest when I gave it one last look. I let my eyes drift over the dragon. Its face was smooth and soft with smaller scales that looked like tiny seashells in a blue sea. When my gaze locked on its vivid violet eyes, I swear I could see sadness. It glanced away and back again, almost pleading. A small chuff escaped its lips like a sob. Beneath me, Tuck sucked in a deep breath and his temperature increased once more. The dragon flinched back, as if knowing another ball of fire was coming its way. And that's when I saw them . . . Two tears the size of basketballs streaming down its cheeks.

I dug my hand into Tuck's feathers. "Stop!"

Alataris yanked the reins to the side and cackled. "Coming to your senses?"

"Not at all." I pressed my thighs into Tuck's sides. "We need to go now."

He turned his head and looked at me with those golden eyes as if I'd lost my mind. Yet when I said nothing more, he tucked his wings into his body and we began to drop down. I looked up at that poor dragon, knowing it was being held against its will like my mother. When its gaze met mine, I saw more tears gathering, as though it was disappointed I didn't fight to help it. My heart broke in my chest, but I didn't know what kind of hold Alataris had on the beast, and I didn't want to hurt it further just to find out. *I'll come back for you.*

The dragon threw its head back and cried out as Alataris brought that whip down again across its tail and sped out of sight.

CHAPTER 11

TUCKER

"What do you mean we can't kill it?" Serrina paced back and forth in front of the book stacks in the back of the library. Her hair was pulled into a high bouncy ponytail that fell down the back of her ripped-up T-shirt. Zinnia's shirt was ripped from battle, but Serrina's was a fashion choice. The rest of my crew sat on either side of the long table that stuck out from the wall like a peninsula.

Zinnia stood off to the side, leaning up against a bookshelf. Her ebony hair was windblown and covered in snowflakes. Tiny icicles hung from the ends. She looked like a dark fae princess with her wide sapphire eyes, pale skin, and pinkened cheeks. Even the snow in her hair looked like a crown. Small rips marred her shirt and leggings, yet she didn't pay them any attention, even when glimpses of her pale skin would peek through. "I'm telling you, I saw it in the dragon's eyes. It did not want to cover the school in ice and snow. Alataris was somehow controlling it, like a slave. We have to free it."

Brax, our tiger shifter, leaned back in his chair and sighed. Though he was the quietest of all the knights, he was also the biggest. In the human world, people would think he was a soldier, with his tight-cut blond hair, camo fatigues, and massive body. "You say you want to do this saving of the dragon, da?"

Zinnia nodded. "Absolutely. It's innocent in all this."

"Then I go." His Russian accent made his words sound so final, as though the decision had been made by all of us. He looked down at himself, studying a patch of small holes in the sleeve of his shirt, then shrugged and faced the rest of us.

A wide smile broke out over Zinnia's face. "Really?"

Brax nodded. "I'm not killing a mythological creature. Not when it can be free."

"Hold up a second." Nova stood and moved beside Serrina. "Don't the rest of us get a say here? I mean, you're asking us to go on a mission to save an ice-breathing dragon that we aren't a hundred percent sure is actually innocent at all. Maybe it likes working for Alataris."

"I'm telling you it wasn't. I saw it in the dragon's

eyes. This was some kind of torture for it. And when Tuck spat flames at it, it cried." Zinnia crossed her arms over her chest. "We have to do something."

The thought of making anything cry, let alone a hulking dragon, made me shift uncomfortably in my chair. What could we do in this situation? Half the queens wanted to just kill it and be done. The other half wanted to risk their lives to free it, if indeed it wanted to be free. I was torn, but deep down I could feel Zinnia's feelings seeping into my body. I knew the mark on my wrist matched hers perfectly, and the longer we were together, the more I would feel her emotions and she would feel mine. My only question was, how much more could I draw this out to keep it a secret? She was mine, and I was hers . . . she just didn't know it yet.

As I sat there looking at her and feeling what she felt, I knew I had to do something to help the dragon. If I didn't, she would go on her own. Of that I was sure. As the leader of the entire crew, it was my job to not only protect the queens, but also to decide what missions we would undertake. But feeling Zinnia's emotions made me want to give in to what she wanted. I leaned back in my chair. *Follow my heart or my head?*

Before I said anything, all eyes were on me. "Well, let's think about this. If we kill the dragon—"

"No one better touch *my* dragon. If any of you harm

one little scale on its head, you'll be answering to me."
Taliam, one of the Fallen who worked along with
Matteaus, barged through the door in all his rocker
glory. His large black wings were tucked in close to his
back. Each feather was tipped with dark green. Taliam
wasn't as hulking as Matteaus. He was all long, lean
muscles and stood only a few inches taller than me. He
wore a black tank top like Matteaus', but rather than
black fatigues, he had on loose-fitting leather pants and
biker boots with thick silver studs around his ankles.
Leather holsters crisscrossed over his chest, and two
sword handles peeked out from between his neck and
wings. His silver hair was shaved tight to the sides of his
head and was longer on the top with strands flopping
over. I'd heard long ago Taliam's hair changed color at
will. Seeing it now, I had a feeling that was true.

How does one greet a supernatural being who was as
old as time itself? *Do I rise and bow? Do I stay seated? I
have no idea.*

I rose to my feet and walked up to Taliam, then
extended my hand to him. "Mr. Taliam, pleasure to meet
you."

"Yeah, it's just Taliam." He rubbed his fingers over the
dark stubble on his jaw, then grabbed my hand and gave
it a quick shake.

The queens, Ashryn, and Adrienne, all sat gaping at

him. Even Zinnia's interest was piqued by him. *I'm not jealous, not one little bit . . . nope, not at all.* "The dragon is yours?"

Taliam shrugged. "Sort of, but you cannot kill or hurt that dragon. The fate of the world, not just Evermore, depends on her survival."

Zinnia arched an eyebrow at him. "Her?"

"Yes, her. If there were only boy dragons, then we wouldn't have more dragons in the world, now would we?" He glanced around at us all gathered together. "This is an interesting court for this cycle."

Interesting good or interesting bad? What did that mean? "What do you mean?" It was odd for him to be standing in the library with us. For starters, he rarely appeared in the Academy and then to just show up. All kinds of warning signs were going off in my mind.

Taliam waved my question away. "Doesn't matter. You all are going to save my dragon, or you'll be answering to the Fallen directly."

"Excuse me, but why can't you help us save her? I mean, she is your dragon." Zinnia stepped away from the book stacks she leaned up against and rested her hands on her hips. The others sucked in shocked breaths. No one, not even a queen, questioned the Fallen.

A light chuckle escaped Taliam's lips, and he pointed

toward Zinnia. "I like her. The answer is simple and yet complicated at the same time. Because, sweet. The long and short of it is, if the Creator doesn't command my interference, then I may not interfere."

Zinnia leaned toward him. "But what if—"

"The time for questions is over. You're all off to Alaska. Pack your bags. It's going to be a chilly ride." He gave a mock salute and headed for the door. Without turning around, he called over his shoulder, "Don't fail. You'd hate to see me when I'm angry. Oh, and I'll have a friend meet you where the Bering Glacier meets the sea in two hours."

Zinnia's eyes widened. "Two hours? We're going to get across the entire country in two hours?"

"I've got this covered." Beckett rose to stand beside her. "I'll portal us there. Nova, I'm gonna need your help to be able to picture where we need to go, okay?"

"Yeah, okay." Nova sagged against Serrina's side. She cast her eye to the floor. The curtain of her white blond hair fell over her face, hiding the way she was biting her lip a second ago. She tugged her elbow-length red gloves farther up her arms. "I haven't been home since I got here."

I knew Nova hadn't seen her family in a while. She didn't really talk about it all that much and I never pressed the subject. Now looking at her nervous face, I knew I should have. "Nova, are you gonna be okay with going?"

Her head snapped up, and she pursed her lips. "Yeah, it's going to be fine." She made a beeline for the door without another word.

Note to self: next time, ask in private.

Adrienne raised her hand, drawing my attention to where she sat between Brax and Ashryn. Her long, thin braids hung down from her head in a waterfall of shining ebony that matched her skin perfectly. When her midnight gaze met mine, I could see the concern in them. "I don't think all of us can go. I mean, have you looked outside? It's not just the school covered in snow. It's the whole New England area, the city, and Jersey. Some of us are going to have to stay behind and help with damage control."

She was right, but there was also another reason I wanted her to stay. We only had four out of five queens we needed to defeat Alataris. Ophelia, the Queen of Spells, had already fallen under Alataris' rule, and now Niche was trying to substitute her with Adrienne, one of the knights. She was brilliant and formidable. As the daughter of Athena, she was even able to do a little magic. For the sake of us all, she had to stay behind and continue her training while helping out. "I agree. Adrienne, you'll stay behind. Anyone else willing to stay?"

She nodded then elbowed Brax in the side. He shrugged. "What? I want to go and save the dragon."

"You're one of the strongest. Reason dictates you stay to help me deal with the pile of crap all around here." When she gave him her bright smile, I knew he was a goner. Our gentle giant couldn't say no when someone truly needed him.

He sighed and leaned his head down on the table. "Fine. I'll miss seeing the big ice dragon. But you owe me one."

Adrienne raised her eyebrows. "I owe you an ice dragon?"

"No, you owe me a visit to see the ice dragon once they save it." Brax rose to his feet and offered Adrienne his hand. "Come, we go see what needs to be done."

"Before you go, keep in mind the rest of us who are outside of the school will be able to be reached by cell . . . hopefully." I gazed out at my crew, knowing we were about to do something dangerous that some of us might not come back from. When my eyes landed on Zinnia, my heart shuddered just thinking about losing her. No. I had to keep my head in the game, though she was my greatest distraction. "Go and pack. We'll meet in the courtyard in an hour and a half. Backpacks only, people. This isn't a vacation."

CHAPTER 12

GRAYSON

I paced back and forth outside of Zinnia's dorm room. Inside, I could feel her nervous energy because of our blood tie . . . it was damn exhausting. Whether this little plan I cooked up was going to work or not was yet to be seen. Part of me didn't want to do it now that we had to face the prospect of trying to free an ice dragon from Alataris. Who knew what we would face over the next few days? But then again, when did I ever play anything safe? *Game on* . . . I raised my hand and knocked on the dark wooden door.

"Just a sec," Zinnia's sweet voice called out. I could hear her scrambling about the room. Then the distinct sound of a *thump* then a "damn it" came from the other side of her door. I knew her heart was racing and her secret hope of who it was waiting for her at the door.

"Come on, love. We haven't got all day. We've got to go about rescuing a dragon and all that. Haven't we?"

The noise on the other side of the door stopped. "Grayson?"

"Were you expecting someone else?" I leaned my shoulder up against the doorframe, waiting.

When she yanked her door wide-open, I glanced over her shoulder, noting the utter disaster her room was. "Has your closet had an accident then?"

She stepped into the doorway and pulled the door shut just enough to hide her room but not close it completely. She glanced over my shoulder as though looking for someone else. "What's up? Is everything okay?"

"Um, yes and no. May I come in?"

She pulled the door in a little tighter to her body. "Maybe you could just tell me here."

With my vampire speed, I reached up, pulled the sleeve of her sweatshirt down, then unsnapped the clasp of the bracelet hiding the mark I knew was on her wrist. I held the bracelet up in front of her face and waved it back and forth. Then I pointed toward the mark on her wrist. "Can I come in now?"

Her lips turned down into a frown while she stepped back and held the door open. "It's a mess, but I guess come in."

I walked through the door and was immediately hit with her sweet vanilla sugar scent. All around, clothing littered the bed and the chair for her desk. At the foot of the bed sat a backpack with not a single thing in it. "I thought you were supposed to be packing?"

"I was when you interrupted me." She held her hand out and wiggled her fingers in a come-hither motion. "Can I have my bracelet back now?"

I dangled the silver chain in front of her face. A tiny phoenix was at the center of it with a sapphire perched in the belly of the phoenix. *Marking your territory, Tuck?* I dropped the bracelet into her outstretched hand. "You do realize what you're hiding, don't you?"

She narrowed her eyes at me. "Not at first, no."

"Do you know who it is?" It was crucial for me to know if she knew who her soul mate was. Based on the feelings she'd been sharing with me through our blood tie, I thought she didn't know or understand who it was.

She shook her head. "I just stepped into this world last week, Gray. I barely know what's going on with my own powers, let alone anyone else's. And I'm guessing it's a soul mate mark because my mother . . ." She choked up for a second, then cleared her throat. "My mother used hers to distract Alataris."

I motioned for her to give me her wrist. "Let's see it then."

Zinnia turned her face away and extended her arm out to me. The soul mate mark was thin and looked like a bunch of infinity signs all connecting together with tiny drops of silver in each circle. I turned her wrist over in my hands, studying it. Before I could let go, she yanked her hand away. "I think you've seen enough. Is it what I think it is?"

"Oh yeah, love. You've got yourself a soul mate all right."

"Wonderful." She shook her head and sighed. "Why are you here, Gray?"

"First, to help you pack." I sped around her room, tossing all the clothing and supplies she'd need for the trip to Alaska. Once everything was neatly folded on the bed next to her backpack, I lay out on her bed with my hands behind my head and my legs crossed at my ankles. Zinnia's bed was surprisingly cozy, with a fluffy black and white comforter, plush pillows, and soft sheets. "Now, like I was saying, I have a proposition for you."

Zinnia stomped over to the bed and began slamming her things into the bag. "You mean, besides going through my underwear drawer? There is such a thing as privacy, Gray."

I could feel her annoyance churning inside of her.

"Oh, I'd love to give you privacy. Believe me. But there's this little issue between us . . ."

Zinnia gasped and took a step back, clutching her wrist to her chest. Her eyes darted around the room like she was looking for an escape. "It's not you . . . is it?"

"Ugh, don't look so put out." With both hands I fluffed the pillow behind my head. "I'm a catch."

Her brows furrowed, and a sick green look came over her face. "Then it is you?"

"Psh, don't flatter yourself, love. Generally speaking, soul mates are within the same species in Evermore. So, unless you've got a pretty little set of fangs hiding behind those boring teeth of yours, I'd say you don't meet my criterion for a soul mate. Plus, there's that pesky little bit of my family curse you wouldn't get by. No, sweet, I am not your soul mate. But I know a way to figure out who is."

I already knew who her soul mate was. It was obvious she and Tuck were meant for each other.

"You said he'd have to be in my own species. That means it'd have to be one of the boys in my craft classes or Beckett." She wrinkled her nose, and I swear I could almost taste the disappointment rolling off her.

"I'm not sure. I think this cycle is changing things up. I know you're disappointed it's not me. But it could be someone outside of the witch casts. There's only one way to find out who it is for sure, though."

Zinnia arched her eyebrow at me. "Now this I've got to hear."

"Basically, you should be my girlfriend." I gave her a toothy smile and waited for her jaw to snap shut.

Five long minutes later, Zinnia shook herself. "Wait, say what now? But you just said—"

"That I wasn't interested in you. I mean, you're beautiful and all that." Her cheeks burned bright red. I ignored it and continued. "But you belong to someone else, and frankly, I think it's about time you found him."

"What's in this for you?" She zipped her backpack shut and pulled on her fur lined thick black leather coat. Large buttons ran down the front of her in two identical rows, and the coat cinched in tight at her waist. Then she pulled a sapphire-colored hat over her head that matched her eyes perfectly.

I rose from her bed and scrubbed a hand over the back of my neck. "Yeah, about that. We might've formed a tiny little"—I coughed into my fist—"blood tie."

She froze while pulling on a black leather glove. "Blood what?"

"Well, you see, after you, you know, healed me the other day, I might have completely *unintentionally*, through no fault of my own, formed a blood tie with you."

"Spit it out now, Gray. What exactly does that mean?" She pulled her backpack over her shoulders and faced me.

"It means I can feel all your emotions . . . like, all of them. And the way I figure it, if you act like my girlfriend, then we can hide that little fact better as well as smoke out who your real soul mate is."

Zinnia stood with her fists at her sides. She held her breath . . . and held it . . . and held it. Her fury smacked into me in wave after wave. "Grayson Shade, I have no idea how the hell this happened, but you make it unhappen right now. Do you hear me? Right now!"

"I can't. It has to wear off on its own." I shrugged.

"How long?" She stomped her foot.

I held my hand out in front of me, trying to calm her down. I lowered my voice to a whisper. "I don't know."

Zinnia dropped her bag on the ground and marched over to a bookshelf full of textbooks from the school. She pulled one off the shelf, thumbed through it, and then tossed it into a pile on the floor. I rose from the bed and walked over to her. "Bit late to be studying, no?"

"Oh, I'm not studying. I'm looking for a spell." She pulled another book down.

I looked up at the two large bookcases that stood

side by side in her room. After only being here for less than a week, she'd nearly filled them all. "What kind of spell?"

She slammed the book in her hands shut and leaned toward me. "The kind of spell that'll turn you into a frog or a pig or some animal I can put in a cage!"

A nervous ball formed in my throat. I'd never seen her so angry before. "That's a little hasty, I think."

She spun on her heels and began digging through the piles of papers on her desk. "I know it's here some-where." She scooped up a pile of papers and looked through those. "And no, I don't think it's hasty. I've been here for all of a few days. I'm having a hard enough time fitting in with the others and now this."

She threw the stack up into the air. The loose-leaf papers fluttered around us, falling to the ground one by one. I could feel anxiety rolling off her so much it nearly choked me. I didn't know how to comfort her. She jabbed her finger in my chest. "No one knows about this, Gray. Do you hear me? The last thing I need is for anyone to know I've formed a blood tie with you. It's difficult enough not controlling my powers fully and everyone being afraid of me. I don't need this too."

I nodded. "I get it, and I promise I won't tell anyone."

"Swear it on this blood tie thingy." She motioned to my body like it was all my fault. In reality it was a complete accident, but if it made her feel better, I would do it.

"What does swearing it on our blood tie accomplish? Rather odd, don't you think?"

"I don't know, but if you tell anyone, then in my mind I'll believe it'll boil your blood or something." She bounced around from one foot to the other. Her energy was all over the place, full of panic and worry. She shook her hands out. "Just do it, it'll make me feel better."

I nodded. "I swear no one will find out."

A knock on the door sounded, and I froze in place. Zinnia pressed her finger to her lips, then mouthed the words *shut up.* I pressed my lips together and nodded. She sighed. "Who is it?"

"It's Tuck. You all set?"

Her heart sped, and excitement coursed through her body at the sound of his voice. *Bloody hell, women can feel every emotion in a matter of moments.* If I didn't find it so cute, I might vomit. Still, I said nothing. Those two needed to be pushed together. Tuck didn't know it, but I knew what his life was like before he became a knight. He deserved a little happiness, and she was just the girl to bring it to him. He just had to get out of the way of himself. *Forbidden rules be damned.*

"Um, yeah. I think so." She glanced around the room.

"Oh, um, I was going to see if you need any help?"

Oh, enough of this already. I sauntered over to the door. Behind me, Zinnia scrambled to stop me, but I was faster. I yanked the door open and smiled brightly at Tuck. "Think we've got it all figured out here."

Tucker stepped back with a small gasp. "Oh, Gray. Didn't know you were here." He wiped the shock from his face, then looked over my shoulder at where Zinnia stood, then back at where I stood. When he narrowed those honey-colored eyes at me, I knew my plan would work. I just needed Zinnia to be in on it.

I hurried to her side, then grabbed her arm and hustled her forward. "Yep, she just needed a bit of help packing. Isn't that right?" I ran back to where her back-pack lay on the floor, plucked it up, and handed it to her.

Zinnia hesitated a moment, glancing from Tuck at me and back again. "Yeah, sure." She took the bag from my hand and hiked it up on her shoulder.

"Oh, I see." Tucker turned around and strode down the hallway, then called over his shoulder, "We leave in ten minutes."

I wrapped my arm around Zinnia's neck. "So you in or you out?"

She tugged my arm over her head and placed it back at my side. Then she jabbed her finger in my face. "I am in until this thing wears off. And you better tell me the second it does. As much as I want to know who my soul mate is, I'm not sure making whoever it is jealous of us is going to work."

"Oh, my dear Zinnia, the things you don't know about men."

She slammed her door shut behind us and rounded on me. "What's that supposed to mean?"

"It means what's mine is mine. Jealousy isn't rational. It's primal. And in Evermore, the primal rule. Just you wait and see. I promise you'll have him soon enough."

Zinnia rolled her eyes. "I don't know how I get talked into this crap. But I swear if you tell anyone it's fake, I will drop you in a den of Alataris' sirens and leave you there."

CHAPTER 13

ZINNIA

I can't believe I agreed to this. As if we didn't have enough going on, I decided to run a scheme with Grayson. *What am I thinking?* I had a list a mile long of things that needed to be done: learn to be a witch, go to Alaska, meet Taliam's friend, save the ice dragon, save my mom, defeat Alataris, and now be Gray's fake girlfriend. Though I had no idea who we were meeting, if it would be dangerous, how we would save the dragon, or find my mom . . . and defeat Alataris, because generations of witches hadn't been able to do so. Most of all I wanted to learn to control my powers and be the Siphon Witch everyone expected me to be. But somehow, we would be expected to do it all. *No pressure or anything.*

I gave Grayson a little shove. "I just need a minute. I'll meet you in the courtyard."

"You sure? It could be quite the entrance if we show up together." He wagged his eyebrows at me.

"I think I'm good." I shook my head.

"Suit yourself." He turned and jetted away from me. A slight breeze ruffled my hair when he passed by me.

I leaned my back up against the wall then closed my eyes and softly banged my head up against it over and over again. *What am I going to do?* A light touch brushed on my shoulder and I startled.

"My dear, I didn't mean to frighten you." Professor Davis stood beside me looking just the way she did on the first day I'd met her. Puffs of her salt and pepper hair stuck out from under a multicolored knitted hat. When she looked up at me with her round brown eyes, I suddenly felt guilty for her seeing me like this.

"Professor Davis." I plastered a smile onto my face. "Hi."

"Hello." She stood with her hands folded in front of her. She wrung her fingers together and shifted from one foot to the other.

When she didn't say anything else, I pushed a lock of hair behind my ear. "Did you want to tell me something?"

"Well, I wanted to give you this." She pulled a book from inside the folds of her dress and handed it over to me.

The cover was a hunter green and frayed at the corners. I could tell from the broken in binding that it was well loved. On the front, in golden scrolling letters it read "Spelling out Spells." I ran my fingers over it. "Thank you so much."

Professor Davis placed her hand on the top of the book. "It taught me well and now I think it'll help you find your way." She stepped in close to me. "You have a rare gift, my dear. I believe with even just a little bit of knowledge that gift will bloom."

I pressed the book to my chest and held it tight. "This means so much."

"You have a long road ahead of you." She patted me on the shoulder. "Best you be prepared."

Before I could say anything else, she gave my arm a little squeeze and wandered away from me. I quickly pulled my backpack around and slid the book inside. This was going to be a long mission and I needed all the help I could get. I sucked in a deep, chilly breath and headed down the hall toward the courtyard where the others would be waiting for me.

STANDING in the courtyard under the continual snow-fall, I wondered how the hell we were going to do it all. The queens were all decked out in full winter gear. Nova wore the least with only a light jacket and a pair of jeans and white snow boots that laced all the way up to her knees. Beside her, Serrina wore a bright red puff jacket that matched her lips. The gray hat she had on her head hung to the side with a fuzzy puff ball on it. Big blond streaked curls hung down her back.

Tucker strolled up behind me and came to stand at my side. I couldn't help but look him over. He had only his leather jacket, black jeans, and combat boots. Flakes of snow dotted his dark auburn hair, and his smoldering eyes almost glowed against the snowy scene that was Evermore Academy.

I turned and looked him up and down. "Aren't you going to be cold?"

"Phoenix." He narrowed his eyes at Gray, then smiled. "I'm hotter."

Grayson, the ever-doting *boyfriend*, stood at my other side. He too wasn't in winter gear. Instead, he wore his traditional black suit coat with dark jeans and snow boots. I motioned to his outfit. "Do you have some kind of inner inferno we all don't know about?"

"Oh, I'm pretty sure you know how hot I am." Gray winked at me. When I glanced back at Tucker, I thought I saw the muscle in his jaw ticking. Yet his face was completely calm and impassive, as if he hadn't heard a word Gray said.

Heat rushed to my cheeks, and I turned to face where Beckett stood in the middle of the courtyard. This whole being Gray's girlfriend couldn't be over soon enough. Instead, I focused my attention on the task at hand. We were all lined up in a U-shape that Beckett stood in the center of. Beside him was Tabi in a bright green snowsuit. She bounced and rubbed her hands together, waiting for him to open the portal.

Beckett motioned for Nova to join him. "I need you to come here so I can see where we're going."

She nodded and took her place beside him, but then he turned to look at me. "Zinnia, can you come and transfer her vision to me?"

Say what now? I stumbled forward. "Um, I think so?"

I'd barely trained with my powers, and now I was fully expected to know them completely. I guess when we were forced into these situations, I had no other choice. I took a deep breath, feeling my powers rise inside of me. They were always there, simmering below the surface, ready for me to use. I pushed them out and flexed them like a muscle. Slivery magic ran down my arms and swirled around my fingertips.

"Just don't knock me out," Nova snapped before turning back to Beckett.

Um, ouch! "I'll try not to." I reached out and placed my hand on her shoulder. My magic swirled around her. "Push your picture out toward me."

When I opened my senses, I immediately saw the shoreline where the glacier met the sea. Out in the middle of the water sat a large glacier surrounded by rough water. The sky was a dark ominous gray, and the waves around the ice were rocking so high no ship would ever go through it. My view was from the shoreline where a pebble beach held no sunshine and each stone looked blacker than the next. The snow-covered forest rose up on all sides, and each tree limb was covered in a layer of green moss then white ice. Fog rolled between the thick tree trunks and over the rough ocean. I reached out and put my other hand on Beckett's shoulder. My magic laced around his body in a line of silver glitter. I forced the image from my mind into his.

His back bowed for a second before he straightened his stance. "Gently, Zin."

"Sorry." I tugged back at the thought I was forcing into him.

He sighed. "Much better."

He cupped his hands one over the other, then slowly expanded them outward until there was an oval-shaped blue magic ball in his palm. He expanded it until he was able to throw it like a disk to stand on its own in the center of the courtyard. I dropped my hands from their shoulders and called my magic back into myself. As the slivery streams disappeared, I took my place next to Gray. I'd never walked through one of Beckett's portals. Crashed a car through one yes, but actually walked, no. Would it be different than the one I'd experienced at the Academy? I had no idea what to expect. I'd only ever been through the school portal, and it was the one that led to Hexia, which looked like a pool of water and felt like walking through calming waves. But this was completely different. To me, Beckett's portal looked more like a mirror with a smooth shimmering blue surface. I could see the scene Nova pictured on the other side. Did that mean it'd be like stepping through a door?

Tucker walked up next to the portal, then turned to face us all. "Right. Grayson, you're through first. Followed by Ashryn, Serrina, Nova, Tabi, and Zinnia. Beckett and I will follow up the end."

One by one we lined up as Tucker specified. Above, the snow began to fall even heavier, coating my jacket, hat, and the long black strands of my hair that fell past my shoulders. As it came to be my turn, he reached out and placed a hand on my shoulder. When I looked up into his honey eyes, they were liquid heat, and I felt an instant pull toward him. I wanted to lean into him. I wanted to place my hand on his stomach and tug him in for a hug. I needed him by my side right now.

As if he knew what I thought, he whispered low enough for only me to hear, "I'll be right behind you."

I nodded and sucked in a deep breath, then stepped into the portal. If I thought it was going to be like walking through a door . . . I was so wrong. The moment I put my foot through, I was sucked in, my body stretched like I was made of putty. It didn't hurt, per se, but felt more like I was literally being put through the wringer. Dizziness overwhelmed me as my body twisted and turned, trying to find a way through this. Like a cannon ball, I shot out of the other end of the portal. My feet flew over my head. My arms pinwheeled and I smacked into the others like a bowling ball, taking them all down with me.

I groaned. "Ugh, sorryyyy."

The wind whipped my hair across my face, blinding me. Overhead, snow fell at a steady clip, coating me before I could open my eyes. I was sprawled flat on my back with people squirming underneath me. Tabi wriggled around at the bottom of the pile laughing so hard I thought she might break something.

I crawled off her as quickly as I could. "How could you be laughing at a time like this?"

I reached down and helped her to her feet.

She sprang up quickly and dusted herself off. "Because I did the same thing." The wind blew so hard I could barely hear her.

I prepared for Tuck to come catapulting through like Tabi and I had, but when his black combat boot came through like it was no big deal and he gracefully walked up to me, I nearly rolled my eyes. Was there anything he couldn't do?

As I gazed out over the water, a heavy fog began to roll in. The waves that pelted the shoreline subsided and smoothed to a glassy surface. The snow that'd been falling continually suddenly suspended in midair, and the wind instantly died. I reached out and poked one of the flakes with my fingers. It slowly drifted away. I'd once seen astronauts letting things float in space. Standing here now in the middle of such utter stillness, it reminded me of them.

Tucker summoned his swords to his hands. Flames shot from his shoulders all the way down to the tips of his swords. "Get ready."

One day I'd ask him how he managed to run those flames all over his body and not burn his clothing off. All of the others around me gathered their magic and unsheathed weapons. I too gathered my magic at the center of my palm, ready to protect them. The sea parted in front of me. Two parallel walls of water stood twisting back like horizontal tornados. Within each one, the water churned and splashed. There in the dead center of those walls was a towering man, wearing nothing but tight wetsuit pants that looked like black and blue fish scales.

Water sloshed down his body, causing his long dark hair to cling to his neck and down his shoulders. In one hand he held a trident. The gleaming silver metal spiraled up to three separate points. Within the trident, bright blue flecks of wavering sea glass sparkled with aqua-colored magic. His face was all angles, with a straight nose, sharp jawline, and high cheekbones. He was compelling in a way my mind couldn't understand.

"Damn," Tabi whispered under her breath.

I had to agree. This man was beautiful and deadly all at the same time. Tucker immediately extinguished his swords and sent them back to wherever he summoned them from.

He stepped out in front of the group. "Greetings, Poseidon."

My eyes widened. *Poseidon! Holy hell.* The *Poseidon.* This was a man who was so legendary even the human world knew who he was and the power he wielded.

Poseidon waved his hand to the side. "Weapons down, children."

The magic I gathered in my hands drifted away on a

breeze, without my commanding it to. *The power of this guy.* He twisted the trident in his hand, and a surfboard made of water rose up under his feet. He stood still as a statue as he torpedoed toward the shoreline. The muscles down his stomach and arms rippled while he kept his balance. When he reached the shore, he leapt off the board and skidded to a halt, sending pebbles flying at our feet.

He tossed his long hair over his shoulder as he approached Tucker. He held his hand out. "Tucker Brand, I saw you in the trials . . . impressive."

Was I the only one who thought this was the weirdest thing ever? We were standing here talking to freaking Poseidon. Well, Tucker was.

He took Poseidon's hand and shook it firmly. "Thank you."

Poseidon glanced over his shoulder and looked directly at me. When I gazed into his eyes, they wavered like rough seas and changed colors from the deepest greens to the most vivid aqua all in the beat of a moment. He winked at me. "So we now have the Siphon Witch."

I cleared my throat. "It's nice to meet you, P-Poseidon."

He canted his head to the side, looking me up and

down. "Powerful and beautiful." His eyes roamed from Gray to me and then to Tuck. "Very interesting."

My eyes widened, and all speech left my body. Before I could muster up an answer, Tucker stepped to the side, blocking his view of me. "We've been sent here by Taliam to save his dragon."

"You and me both." He rolled his eyes and waved us forward. "Come on."

"Come where?" I stepped from around Tucker and gazed out over the sea. "Into the water?"

I'd once heard that the water in Alaska grew so cold in the fall and winter months that if a person fell into it, hypothermia would set in immediately, killing whomever it was that fell in.

Poseidon looked over his shoulder and met my eye. "If you want to know why Taliam needs this dragon, then yes, into the water. Don't worry, witch. I'll keep you safe."

I stepped forward into the water.

CHAPTER 14

ZINNIA

As I followed behind Poseidon, Tucker came to my side and leaned in close to my ear. "Careful."

I nodded without saying a word to him. I knew the Greeks were tricky supernaturals. Even Matteaus had mentioned how much of a pain in the ass they were to him and the other Fallen. They all claimed to be gods among men, but in reality, they were just very powerful. As I stepped forward, the water rose up over the soles of my shoes. The cold seeped into my feet, and a shiver ran over my body.

I whispered to Tuck, "I don't know about this."

"Just be ready for anything."

"Not to worry. I've got your back," Gray added as he took up a spot on the other side of me.

Really, dude? Now? You have to add that in now? I rolled

my eyes and felt the magic rise within me, ready to be used at any moment.

Once all of us stepped within the water walls, they rushed toward us, closing up quickly. "Um, Poseidon?"

"Relax, little witch." He tossed his hand over his shoulder. The second the water was about to smack into us and send us sprawling, it slammed into an invisible barrier. It swarmed over us but never touched us. We were in some kind of air bubble.

"Now I know what the people of Atlantis must feel like." We floated along in the rough, murky seas. I could barely make out Poseidon, who swam just in front of our bubble. The deeper we went, the more pressure I felt coming down on us. My ears popped.

Tuck stiffened beside me. "I don't like this."

"Me neither." I cupped my hands against the bubble, but the water was so dark it was hard to make out anything. Then the temperature dropped even more. My breaths came in white puffs of smoke.

"Tuck, can't you heat us up?" Beckett called from just behind Nova and Serrina, who huddled together, shivering.

He shook his head. "Do you really want to test the limits of the bubble and fill it up with hot air when the water temperature is well below freezing?"

Then the murky haze started to thin. The water

cleared just enough that I could see through it. Tiny particles floated in front of us. The water was a deep green and the sand from the bottom of the sea slowly drifted back into place.

"There. What is that?" I pointed toward the glacier.

Only, it wasn't what I expected a glacier to be under water. I thought it'd be like watching ice float in a glass of water, all white crystallizations and points of clear I could see through. No, something was very off about this glacier. There in the middle of it was an enormous form. Chunks of ice broke off from the glacier and floated around the bottom of it. As we came in closer, I saw he was a giant, a literal giant trapped within the ice itself. His skin was a dark green sludge color. Jagged red lightning-shaped lines ran down his arms and across his bare torso. His head was bald and block-like. His eyes were closed as though asleep, but I could see the muscles in his body twitching and moving.

Poseidon pointed to his hand where the ice was the thinnest. Another large chunk broke off, and the water rippled with power. The bubble tilted and spun.

My stomach rolled, and I pressed my hand over my mouth. "Okay, let's not do that again."

The giant's head was cube-like, with his grotesque square jaw jutting out past his upper lip. Something was happening. I could feel its power shifting, rising even more.

I glanced around at the others, who stood pressed against the bubble in awe. "Do you guys feel that?"

They all shook their heads. Tucker looked down at me. "Feel what?"

"We need to leave now, Tucker. Now!" I pressed against the back of the bubble and braced myself. The building power was so intense it seeped into my body, mixing with my own magic. Suddenly, the sea had a pulse, a heartbeat I could feel and control as if it were my own. My head shot up, and I gazed at the giant. His eyes flashed wide-open. There were no pupils or irises, just pure blackness. Air bubbles the size of boulders rose from his nose.

I ran forward and banged on the bubble. "Poseidon! Look!"

Just as the Greek's head whipped up, a large chunk of ice broke off the giant's arm. He swung it forward and smacked into Poseidon, sending him reeling out of sight.

And then the bubble burst.

CHAPTER 15

ZINNIA

Water rushed into my face. I sucked in one gasping breath before I was thrown back into the ice-cold sea. My body instantly seized up. My arms and legs felt heavy, and I couldn't move them. I tried to kick to the surface, but we were so far down there was no way I'd make it up with soggy clothes and boots filled with water. Haziness dragged me under, and I let it. The cool seeped into me, lulling me into a peaceful drifting. I wanted to let it take me, to give into the dark abyss where my lungs didn't burn for air and water didn't fill my mouth and nose as I gasped and failed to fight even for a second.

A warm object speared around my waist. Heat, precious heat, radiated all over my body. *Tucker!* I could suddenly move my arms and legs. I didn't hesitate. I gathered all my magic around me and pulled from whatever power the giant had over the water. Silver streams lit up the murky darkness, and I forced the water away from me, reforming the bubble Poseidon had used on us. Tucker was wrapped around my waist. We both sucked in gasping breaths as we lay on the bottom of the bubble in a sprawling heap.

He rolled over on all fours and coughed up water. "We"—gasp—"have"—cough—"to   get"—gasp—"the others."

I couldn't answer him between my breaths. I closed my eyes and sent streams of my magic through the water like octopus arms. I didn't know what I was doing. All I knew was I had to help them all somehow. With my instincts going on nothing but adrenaline, I focused my magic and connected with the ocean the way the giant was. I felt their lives seeping away like a gift to the sea. I wrapped a water tentacle around the first person I felt and dragged them forward into the bubble. Gray fell to the floor in a soggy heap. Three more tentacles and Serrina, Nova, and Ashryn were lying on the floor at my feet, shivering and barely breathing, but alive.

Tucker rose to stand and brushed gentle flames over all of them, drying their clothing and warming them while not burning anyone. I started sending my magic tentacles out farther, looking for Tabi and Beckett. "Shit, Tuck. I-I can't find them!"

He rested his hand on my shoulder. "You're doing all you can, Zin. Breathe."

But I couldn't breathe. Panic overcame me, and my heart raced. The longer they were out in that freezing water, the more of a chance they wouldn't make it. Tears prickled the backs of my eyes, and I spun in a circle, sending my magic out even farther. A body came surging at us, then Tabi dove through the bubble I created to land on the floor next to Serrina. She looked better than all the others. The water had barely affected her. She was the Queen of Elements, so she'd fared much better than the rest.

She huddled in on herself, shaking. "That water is deadly."

"Beckett!" I didn't know why I screamed or if he would indeed hear me, but I had to find him.

Tabitha shot to her feet. "You haven't found him?"

I shook my head and turned to face her. "Help me, Tabi." I grabbed the tops of her arms and shook her. "Please."

She closed her eyes, and I felt her magic slip into my body. Yellow light flooded out and surrounded us. I knew where every life was, felt every fish and every move the ocean made. I drew more magic from the giant and used everything I had in me to find Beckett. A wave rippled out from our bubble, and there, over a hundred yards away, I found him floating. I couldn't feel his pulse through the water like I could the others. He didn't move. I quickly wrapped one of my magic tentacles around his waist and tugged him toward us. His body fell onto the floor of the bubble like a dead fish. Water seeped from his blue lips in a stream.

"Oh God!" I dropped to my knees beside him and pressed my hands to his chest, one over the other, and began pumping them up and down the way I'd learned in my first aid class. Still nothing from him. "It's not working. Oh God. Breathe, Beckett! Breathe!"

I shoved my hands down on him harder. Tucker dropped to his knees behind me and wrapped his arms around my waist to pull me back. I shoved at him. "No, no! He's not dead."

I scrambled back over his body and pulled Tabi down next to me. "Get the water out of his lungs!"

She nodded. "Give me a boost."

This time, I shoved my magic into her, giving her more power. She held her hands over Beckett's body. Yellow streams of light shot from her fingertips into his mouth. His back bowed up off the ground as each and every drop of water came up his throat and out of his mouth. His eyes flashed wide-open, and he rolled to his side, curling into the fetal position as he coughed and gagged.

Before I said a word, Tucker looked down at him. "This is going to hurt, dude . . . bad."

He lifted his hands over him, and heat fired out from his palms. The air in the bubble became as hot as a sauna, and sweat beaded my brows. On the ground, Beckett threw his head back and screamed.

I grabbed onto Tucker's shoulder. "What are you doing to him?"

"The hypothermia is too deep in him. I have to warm him up before his heart stops. Think about it. He's nearly freezing. Extreme cold followed by immediate extreme heat is going to hurt."

Beckett's face crinkled in pain. "Stop! Just stop!"

Tucker gritted his teeth. "No."

I pulled Beck's head into my lap and brushed the hair back from his face. "It's almost over." I turned to Tucker. "Isn't it?"

He nodded, then the heat from his hands began to subside to a low warmth that kept the rest of us from freezing. Beckett's features smoothed out, and he sighed, yet his eyes didn't open. The blue tinge that'd stained his lips only moments before was slowly fading away.

I kept patting his hair the way my mother used to do

whenever I didn't feel well. "You're okay, Becks. You're going to be just fine now."

"Oh . . . my . . . God! What is that?" Serrina pointed out toward the glacier. I pressed myself up against the side of the bubble, using all my power to keep it up and surrounding us. Without Poseidon's power over the sea around us, the bubble tossed and turned. Though I tried my hardest to keep it steady, I was no match for Alaska or the giant about to break loose from its ice prison. We spun and tilted like we were on a rollercoaster. The others huddled together on the floor, holding on to each other for dear life.

"Guys, I don't know about you, but I'm thinking if that giant gets out, it's a bad thing." I squinted my eyes, looking at the jet stream of water heading straight at the giant.

Grayson pressed the back of his hand to his mouth. "I need out of here or I'm going to toss it all."

"Shut up, Gray," Tucker snapped, then moved next to me. "It's Poseidon."

Poseidon held his trident, pointing it at the giant's arm, then fired off a jet of ice, coating the loose arm in layer after layer. The water churned violently, tossing us around like a rowboat in the middle of a hurricane. Grayson rushed to my side and placed his hands on my hips, holding me still. I froze in place. His hands felt wrong on me somehow. Like they didn't belong there. *Now? You're going to do this now?*

My eyes shot to Tucker's. He just pressed his lips together and turned to hold Serrina and Nova as best as he could. Beckett continued to lie unconscious on the floor, while Ashryn and Tabi seemed to ride the waves like balance was their natural talent. Poseidon bared his teeth and roared. His mane of black hair drifted around him, and his eyes glowed a shocking green. The trident lit up and shook in his hand. I could feel the vibrations on the side of the bubble. Then a blinding white light blazed out from it, and everything within a one-mile radius froze solid, including the giant . . . and us.

CHAPTER 16

The sea around us froze solid. One second, we were standing in an air bubble, and the next we were in an ice cavern. I dropped my hands from holding on to Serrina and Nova. "Damn it. This can't be happening."

"Tuck, how are we going to get out of here to free the dragon if we are buried miles under ice in a tiny pocket of air?" Zinnia paced back and forth. "Can you melt it?"

I shrugged. "I could try. All I know is we will get out."

Before I could let the flames burn through me to melt the layers over us, a tunnel opened above our heads and the ice beneath our feet shook and groaned. It cracked beneath us, sending small shards skittering across the ground. I threw my hands up. "What now?"

The ice rose into a platform, and we drifted up the

hole above us like riding an elevator. Nova and Serrina pulled Beckett to his feet and wrapped each of his arms over their shoulders.

When his eyes met mine, he gave me a half smile. "I died, didn't I?"

I nodded. "Yep."

My ears popped as we went higher. We passed by large cracks in the ice, all leading back toward the giant. Shards the size of cars fell off one by one, tumbling downward as water rose up beneath the platform we stood on. Frozen mist sprayed us from all directions, as if the water was going to break through at any moment and swallow us whole. Our speed increased, forcing us all to drop down onto our knees under the blistering winds. Just as I was about to light everything on fire to stop the wild ride, the platform came to a sudden halt. We hurdled into the air as though we'd been launched from a catapult. I forced my wings from my back. They exploded in hot, burning flames. I swooped down and caught Zinnia, then dropped her back on the shoreline before I shot back up and caught Nova and Serrina. Tabi had her hands out at her sides and used her wind powers to gently place herself down. Grayson grabbed a hold of Beckett and landed in a crouch with Beckett at his side. Once again, the snow that'd been falling stopped in midair, hanging there like dust particles.

"Is everyone okay?" I landed at the center of them all and spun in a small circle. My crew looked beaten and worn, but we were all still alive. Thanks to Zinnia. I nodded toward her. When she gave me that shy smile of hers, I wanted to walk over to her. I wanted to scoop her up in my arms and press my lips to hers. But I didn't. I held fast, forcing my feet to be glued to the ground.

As Grayson strolled over to her, I had to stop myself from stepping between them. How could he? He knew the rules. Anything between a knight and queen was forbidden, and yet he dared cross that line . . . with her . . . my Zinnia. I didn't know what I was doing, but I took a step toward him. My temper burned like acid in my veins. After all we'd been through, she couldn't be with him. I balled my hands into fists. When he wrapped his hand around her back, I gathered a ball of fire in my palm, ready to launch it at him.

He leaned in closer to her, whispering in her ear. It wasn't his place to be close to her. It was mine. How could this be happening? We all almost died, and he was flirting with her. *No!* I was so close to them I could hear her whispering back to him.

"Ah, you're all alive. Excellent." Poseidon walked across the ice, slow-clapping his hands. "I was sure at least half of you had died."

Rage erupted from me, and flames shot from the

wings on my back, turning the snow around me to watery slush. Though I didn't want to, I turned away from Zinnia and rounded on Poseidon. "No thanks to you."

"Watch your tone, Phoenix," Poseidon snapped.

"Or what? You'll drown us? Too late for that. Or freeze us? Also too late." I crossed my arms over my chest. "Tell us why you took us down there or we are gone."

"Are you demanding things of me?" Poseidon twisted the trident in his hand, and bright magic flickered around it. "Demanding things is not the way to go."

I didn't have time for this. None of us did. We had a dragon to save, not nearly drown and get killed by ice-encased giants. I turned away from Poseidon and snapped my finger at Beckett. "Portal now."

Beckett didn't hesitate. He began gathering his blue sphere of magic in his hand. It was weak at best, and I didn't know if we would be able to get back. But I was done with this little field trip, done risking my crew with no explanations, done nearly dying, and done watching baby leeches hanging all over *my* soul mate.

"Wait," Poseidon called after me.

I spun on my heels and raised my eyebrows. Should I have answered him? Yes. Did I? No. I put my hands on my hips and waited.

Poseidon shook his head. "Let it never be said you aren't a difficult knight."

I met his gaze yet didn't say anything to him. We were here for a reason, and it was time to tell us.

He sighed, then pointed out over the cracking ice. "That giant you all just saw is Karroust."

He paused, waiting for one of us to say something —anything.

Zinnia took a step forward and faced Poseidon with not an ounce of fear on her face. "Who?"

"Tell me you know who I'm talking about." He glanced around at all of us once more. "Karroust." He threw his hands up. "What do they teach you in that damn school?"

He paced back and forth across the beach. The rocky shore crunched under his bare feet as he used his trident like a walking stick. "Karroust is half Titan, half giant. His powers lie in the sea. Evil powers."

"What's he got to do with the dragon?" Grayson again sped to Zinnia's side. Was anyone else seeing this, or was it my jealousy eating at me from the inside out?

"The dragon, Aldesse is her name by the way, is the one who has kept Karroust encased in ice for ages. And now that she's gone . . . we are all in danger." He stopped mid-step and looked directly at Zinnia. "Did you feel his power?"

She nodded. "It was toxic, almost smothering."

"Think of that times a thousand." He turned and met my eye. "If Aldesse isn't returned soon, Karroust will get loose, and if that happens . . . may the Creator help us all."

"How come you can't keep him here?" Even now I knew he couldn't. The water he'd frozen solid was already breaking up like a 7-11 ICEE.

"Isn't it enough of a job for me to control *all* the seas?" He turned toward Tabitha. "Elemental Witch, I need your help."

Tabi pressed her hand to her chest. "Me? Why?"

Poseidon bent low and met her eye. "You, my talented little witch, will help me control the seas while I stand guard and try to keep Karroust contained until the others can rescue Aldesse."

When she glanced over at me, I gave her a subtle nod. The last thing the world needed was a sea giant wreaking havoc on it. I turned and motioned for Beckett. "You'll stay here with her."

Serrina stepped forward. "I'll stay too."

Poseidon wrinkled his nose at her. "You? Why you? The giant doesn't need a crush, little girl."

She crossed her arms over her chest and tapped her foot impatiently. "First of all, ew. Second of all, don't you think dealing with a giant of this power would be a lot easier if he was, say, calm and willing to do whatever you wanted?" At Poseidon's pause, she tilted her head to the side and snapped, "Yeah, that's what I thought."

"Hold on a second." Zinnia held her hands out, stopping everyone else from talking. "What I don't understand is how Alataris got the dragon in the first place. Clearly it's powerful and can defend itself."

"The only way anyone can take a dragon is against its will. He stole the dragon heart scale off of it." Poseidon shrugged, as if this were common knowledge.

I pressed my lips together. "The dragon heart what?"

He rolled his eyes. "Honestly, do they teach you nothing in that school?" The . . . dragon . . . heart . . . scale." He spoke in slow, halted words, as if I were a toddler. "The dragon cannot live without it. That scale protects the dragon's heart, and if Alataris has the heart scale, the dragon is trapped to do his bidding . . . like, oh say, I don't know. Freeze the whole eastern coast."

"Great. So we have to find where Alataris hid the scale before we can even come close to freeing the dragon. Excellent. And how long do we have before the giant unfreezes and the seas go to shit?" I threw my hands up. *Gotta love being a knight.*

"As long as your Elemental Witch can control the water long enough . . ." He started walking backward into the water. Before he dove in backward, he smiled and said, "I'd say four days max . . . good luck."

"Beckett, we're going to need a portal." I turned toward the rest of my crew. "This is going to be a shit show. Ladies, I need each of you to give Zinnia a hit of your powers."

Zinnia's eyes widened. "Wait. What? Why?"

"Because, we are splitting up and we're going to need all the power you can get." I turned and met her eyes. "You can do this."

Without hesitation, the other three queens hit her at the same time. Zinnia levitated off the ground, and her mouth opened in a soundless scream as streams of power filled her. Her hair fanned out around her face. Ribbons of yellow magic flew from Tabi and wrapped around her waist. Purple sparks from Nova danced all over Zinnia's body. Red glittering lines drifted into her nose and mouth. Then as if she'd taken control, all the different colored magic turned into silver swirls that wound around her and disappeared into the palms of her hands. She slowly drifted to the ground, gently touching her feet down to the ground. Her skin shimmered with magic.

She narrowed her eyes at me. "Next time you decide to light me up like a freaking firecracker, how about you ask first . . ."

She walked right past me without stopping and went through Beckett's portal back to the school.

Grayson stopped to stand right next to me. "Yeah, mate. Not cool."

Before he stepped into the portal, her delicate hand popped out, wrapped in his shirt, and yanked him forward to follow her.

Damn it!

CHAPTER 17

TUCKER

Back in the library at school, I couldn't concentrate on anything, not while Zinnia was pissed at me. Though she sat all the way on the other side of the table, I could feel her anger rolling off her in waves. The glow she'd gotten from the infusion of magic lightened to a small hum, but I could feel it crackling around her. Each time she looked at me, she'd narrow her eyes and purse her lips. Gray sat at her side, murmuring things to her. Sometimes her lip would pull up into a half smile. At others, she'd roll her eyes at him. It was killing me not knowing what they were saying or what she was thinking.

"Tucker! Are you with us?" Niche snapped from the head of the table. When I turned to look at her, she stood with her hands pressed to the wooden surface. Her hair, which was normally smoothed back from her face in a tight bun, was falling out in strands around her face. As always, her overly-large glasses slipped down the end of her nose.

I nodded. "I'm with you."

When she raised her eyebrows at me, she might as well have said *yeah right* out loud. "Moving on. I've narrowed the possibilities of where Alataris would be hiding the dragon heart scale down to two places."

"Wait a second. I thought it'd be obvious that he'd have the scale on his floating island with him." Whenever Zinnia spoke, my whole body stood on edge, so aware of every inflection in her tone, of the way she said things and the emotion behind it . . . it was maddening.

Niche nodded. "Logically speaking, yes, but before all of you ascended to become knights and queens, I was studying Alataris for twenty years. And I am one hundred percent sure he wouldn't keep the scale on the island with him. It'd be too easy for a group like us to take it and free the dragon. No, that evil genius has spread himself out."

I leaned over the map she had laid out over the table, though it didn't look like any world map I'd ever seen before. "So, where do you think he's got it hidden?"

"Rumor has it that he keeps a vault hidden some-where in the world." Niche waved her hand over the maps.

"Yeah, that narrows it down a lot, love. Somewhere in the world could be anywhere. How do we find it? And once we find it, how do we break into a centuries-old vault that only has one owner and is magically protect-ed?" Grayson leaned back in his chair and crossed his arms over his chest.

"I wasn't finished, Mr. Shade. Years ago Alataris had, let's say a fling, with a Fury. Rumor had it for decades he trusted her to keep one of his most prized possessions." She pushed her glasses back up her nose.

Ashryn, who sat across from me, looked down at the maps. "You can't possibly want us to go there."

"Go where?" I glanced from Ashryn at Niche.

Niche didn't answer me. Instead, she nodded at Ashryn. "That's exactly what I'm saying. If you knew you were going mad, wouldn't you leave clues for your-self about where you've kept your most important artifacts?"

"Go where?" I insisted, yet they didn't even look at me.

Ashryn's long sandy hair fell over her pointed ears as she nodded. "I would indeed. But what makes you think it's there?"

I shoved my hands in my hair. "Where?"

"I believe he gave her a map with clues on it for safe-keeping. The only thing is, once you give something to a Fury . . . there's no getting it back. Unless she would have a reason to give it up. Like a scorned lover . . ."

Ashryn sat back in her chair. "Interesting theory. Are there truly such things as scorned lovers? In the Windelos, the elf kingdom, we do not have these things. We simply have a battle of either wits or swords to settle our differences."

I glanced over at where Zinnia and Gray sat too close for my liking. *There could indeed be scorned lovers.* It was an interesting theory for sure. "So you want us to go meet this Fury . . ."

"Her name is Tisiphone, yes," Niche finished for me.

"Tisiphone . . . and simply ask her to hand over the map to Alataris' vault?" I tipped my chair back, making it rest on only two legs.

"I'm sure there's something you'll have to negotiate with. But essentially, yes. You need to go to the den of Furies and ask her for it. Actually, Megaera is the lead Fury and she'll have just as much say in this as Tisiphone, her sister. But honestly there is no other way." Niche shrugged.

I held my hand up. "There's one thing you have yet to tell us."

"What's that?"

"Where exactly is the den of Furies, Niche?" I arched my eyebrow and again glanced down at the odd map in front of her.

She reached her arm out over the crinkled browning paper and pointed to a spot on it right in the middle of it. "Right here in the . . ." She paused, looking straight at Nova. "Underworld."

Nova shifted uncomfortably. "Really? We have to go there?"

After learning about all the different casts and what they all represented, I never thought I'd get a Queen of Death who actually didn't like anything about it. She hated Reanimants. Those zombie-like creatures made her gag. She wrinkled her nose at skeletons and squeaked whenever a spirit would speak to her.

Zinnia stood and walked to the other side of the table to stand between Niche and me. When she leaned over the map, her sweet vanilla sugar scent hit me so hard I nearly reached up and wrapped my fingers in the ends of her hair.

She pointed to the same spot on the map. "How exactly do we get down there?" She looked at Nova.

"Oh, don't look at me. It doesn't work like that. The underworld is ruled by Hades and, well, the other one we don't talk about. But yeah, I can only open a door to get down there, but we have to get to a door for me to open."

Zinnia shrugged. "Okay, well, Beckett is still in Alaska helping Tabi and Serrina control the seas and giant. So where is the closest door? Because we only have four days."

Niche zipped over to another bookshelf and pulled an old tome from the stacks. Its red binding was as thick as my thumb and covered in dust. She blew across the top of it, sending dust particles everywhere, before she rejoined us at the table. When she slammed the book down, the noise broke the quiet of the library.

Niche turned to the other students studying across the way, who shot dirty looks at her. "Oops, sorry."

Niche opened the book and thumbed through the pages until she landed on the right one. Then she pressed it flat to the table.

Zinnia read the title out loud. "Entrances to the underworld can be found all over the world. The major ones will be obvious, as the souls who could not pass onto the next life would haunt those places." Her eyes widened. "So we need to find a place that has a history of being haunted?"

Niche nodded. "Yep." She pulled a folded piece of

paper from her back pocket, then handed it to me. "Thanks to Google, this is the place that is the closest to us and is one of the most haunted places in the entire country."

I opened up the paper and read it. "Eastern State Penitentiary in Philly?"

Nova hid her face in her hands. "Ugh, violent spirits. There has to be someplace else."

Niche shook her head. "No place that we can get to in only a few hours. Get ready. There is a bus waiting outside for you all." She held her wrist up and checked the time. "If you leave within the hour, you'll get there just after midnight, which will be perfect."

"Why perfect?" Zinnia had already begun walking to the far end of the table and collected her jacket.

"Because you can't just walk into a tourist attraction in the middle of the day and open a door to the underworld, silly." Niche smiled.

Zinnia chuckled. "Of course. No doors to other worlds should be opened during the day because that would be far less creepy and practical."

Niched began to collect the books and maps up off the table. "Exactly. Okay, off with all of you. The bus will be outside waiting. Good luck." She stuck her hand in her pocket. "Oh, and, Tuck." She tossed a set of keys to me. "Be careful."

I caught them and shoved them in my jean pocket. "I will." I wanted to stay and talk with her longer, but at the same time, I wanted to go after Zinnia . . . Zinnia would always win out.

CHAPTER 18

GRAYSON

The good news? My plan was working accordingly. Tuck was good and jealous. The only problem was Zinnia was so angry at him I could feel it like they were my own feelings. Hell, if I didn't know it was coming from her, I might've slapped the poor sod myself. Even now as we walked side by side toward the courtyard, I could feel her hesitations.

"Gray, I'm not sure this little plan of yours is a good idea."

Behind us, I felt Tucker's nervous energy. If only the two of them could tap into their soul mate bond just as easily. My guess was they overthought every move they made with each other and it stopped them from seeing it all as clearly as I did. The benefits of being a vampire, we were always calm, cool, and collected. Unflappable, even. "I think it's had its benefits."

"I don't even know what you're talking about. Look, we have so much to do now, and this whole thing isn't working for me, okay?"

I stopped in my tracks and turned to face her. "Are you breaking up with me?"

Her mouth dropped open, and she froze. "I-I don't recall us ever saying we were actually dating."

I wrapped my arm around her shoulder and dragged her next to me. "Zinnia, love. You've got to trust your old vampire friend. I know about these things. And I'm telling you this is nothing."

"Beckett almost died, we all nearly drowned, Poseidon is fighting a freaking giant, Taliam has blatantly threatened to throttle us if anything happens to Aldesse, his dragon . . . I mean, don't you think dating seems a bit insignificant at this point?"

She had a very good point.

"Nope."

She threw her hands up. "Honestly, this mark on my wrist or whatever it means can wait."

I still had my arm around her shoulder when I pulled us to a stop. "Imagine, if you will, that we don't make it through this—"

"Yeah, that's not morbid at all." She ducked out from under my arm and pushed it away.

"Just hear me out." I glanced behind us to make sure Tuck hadn't gotten close enough to hear us. "What if you lived the last days of your life never knowing who your heart truly belonged to? I don't know about you, but I'd like to know before I go."

Her sapphire eyes went wide. "Gray, I had no idea you were so . . . romantic."

Me, romantic? No. "What, me? Nooooo. Just doing a friend a solid."

In truth, I was doing it for us all. In the vampire kingdom, soul mates were very rare, but they made each other infinitely more powerful. If we could harness the power Zinnia and Tucker could have, we might stand a chance of winning against Alataris. *Sure, it's for the team, Gray . . . and not even the least bit entertaining . . . not one bit . . .*

Tucker was about ready to pounce, and I didn't want to be here when he did. "Listen, you just wait here for a minute, all right?"

Zinnia looked up and down the hall then out at the courtyard. "I mean, aren't we supposed to"—she pointed toward the front of the school—"you know, get going?"

"I need just a moment to clear my mind." I patted her on the shoulder. "All right, good, yes?"

When I turned away from her, she took a step to follow behind me. I spun around and held my hand up, stopping her.

She looked at me with wide eyes. "Gray, what is wrong with you?"

Tucker popped his head from around the corner, then took a step back into the shadows.

I threw my hands up. "Oh, for Pete's sake, woman. Count to ten then come on."

"What are you—"

"Just do it," I cut her off and whirled around, then strode out into the courtyard into the falling snow.

CHAPTER 19

ZINNIA

I counted to ten just like Grayson demanded me to, then began making my way to the bus. As I walked down the hall of Evermore Academy, I felt the magic the others had shot into me like an extra layer of skin. Pins and needles crawled over me, waiting for me to use it, begging for me to use it. I lifted my hand up and absently twirled my fingers, letting small silvery streams of power wind around my fingertips. Grayson was only a few steps ahead of me, and I stared at his back, trying to calm my angry nerves. How could Tuck have loaded me up like this without a second thought, without even asking? And how could trying to dump my fake boyfriend go so wrong? I was pretty sure I said I wanted to break up and he said no. *Can a person actually say no to breaking up?*

Just as I was about to walk out into the courtyard, I pulled my jacket higher on my shoulders, getting ready to face the snow mounds falling over the courtyard. A warm grip wrapped around my elbow and tugged me sideways into a hidden hallway closet. When the door snapped shut behind me, I was lost in total darkness. The woodsy smell I craved to be around flooded my nose. "Tucker?"

He snapped his fingers, and a small flame hung in the air just beside us like a floating candle. We stood staring at each other. The flame bathed his face in warmth, and I could see the flickering reflected in his honey eyes. A lock of his auburn hair fell across his forehead into his face. My hand twitched to brush it away from his face, yet I stood motionless.

"Hey." His voice was smooth and calm. But when I was this close to him, I could feel the turmoil running through his body. I wanted to pull him into me and wrap my arms around him. But I held myself back even though I didn't want to. That was the way it was every time I was around him. Always wanting more and never getting it.

"Hey." I waited for him to say something else, wanting him to say something else. The tension between us cracked and sparked. "Why am I in a broom closet?"

"Are you with Gray?" The words tumbled from his mouth so quickly I almost asked him to repeat himself.

I wanted to scream that I wasn't, or was I? That I only needed to be with him. "Why do you want to know?"

"Has anyone ever told you answering a question with a question is evasive . . . and frustrating?" He reached out and brushed his hand over the end of a lock of my hair, then wrapped it around his finger and toyed with it. My thick black waves were so dark compared to his pale skin.

"No."

"Well, it is." He took a small step closer. The heat coming off his body seeped into me. "So, are you with him?"

"I can't see how that mat—"

He leaned forward and pressed his lips to mine, cutting off my words and every thought I could possibly have. Electricity shot through my body, and I threw my arms around his neck, pulling him closer. Like two puzzle pieces coming together, we fit perfectly. A low moan escaped my lips. The moment his tongue brushed against mine, my heart leapt into my throat and I pressed my whole body to his.

Tucker ran his hands down my hips. Each of his fingers pressed into me. I wanted him to hold me tighter and never let me go. He stepped in closer, backing me up against the wall. When my back bumped the shelves, I lifted one of my legs and wrapped it around his hip and pulled him closer with it. All the while, he held me to him with one of his hands on my hip and the other wound in my hair.

A deep growl vibrated in his throat. It was primal and called to me in a way I didn't think possible. Heat bloomed in my stomach, and I never wanted this to end, never wanted him to let me go. In that moment wrapped in his arms, with his lips pressed to mine and our tongues wound together, I felt nothing like this ever before. The connection was so strong it nearly staggered me. The world fell away. I forgot all the things that plagued us and only felt him in my arms for a single perfect moment in time . . .

One second his lips were on mine, and the next he pulled away from me. He leapt back and pressed himself against the wall opposite me. His chest heaved up and down as he sucked in deep breaths. He held his hand out in front of him, warding me off as if I were the one who started this. "We can't."

"Why? Because it's *forbidden*? Do you know how stupid that sounds?" I threw my hands up, then turned for the door.

"Zin, please."

I froze with my hand on the doorknob. "Please what?"

"I just . . ." He shoved his hands through his hair and grunted.

"You just what, Tucker?"

"I just can't . . . I can't . . ." The muscle in his jaw ticked as he pulled at his hair.

"Can't what? Say it, Tuck, or I'm leaving now, and I won't look back." As I turned the doorknob, it creaked. It was a warning I meant what I said.

"Ugh, fine. I can't be without you. Okay?" He sucked in a deep breath. "Did you ever stop to think what would happen if we got caught for even a second?"

I dropped my hand, then turned to face him. "Tell me. What would happen?"

"Best-case scenario they send me away . . . and worst . . ." He shivered. "I don't want to think about it."

This was so unfair! Why would I feel this way about him if I wasn't supposed to be with him? Send him away? To where? I didn't know how to deal with this new information or if it even made sense to me. "Then I guess you'd better stay away."

"Zinnia—"

I yanked the door open and stepped out, slamming right into Gray's chest.

His eyes widened, and he raised his eyebrows. "Everything okay, love?"

I shoved by him, my fake boyfriend, to run away from the guy I wanted to be my real boyfriend. I hiked my backpack up on my shoulder and gritted my teeth. "Just fine."

CHAPTER 20

GRAYSON

This is awkward. Bloody awkward. I stood in the doorway of the broom closet, peering at Tucker. The man looked as though he'd just had his life ripped from his hands. Normally, his eyes were a deep honey color. Now they began to bleed red, the way a vampire's did when bloodlust got to be too much. As he sucked in heaving breaths, his body seemed to grow bigger. His muscles strained and bulged while he braced his hands out at his sides and held on to the wooden shelves behind him. He bowed his head, and dark locks of his hair fell into his face. Flames spread from his shoulders down to his hands, lighting up the small space like it was midday.

My heart raced in my chest. He was clearly on the edge of breaking. I knew I shouldn't push him, but part of me just couldn't help it. He made it so easy. I crossed my arms over my chest, then leaned up against the doorframe. "Bad day?"

The shadow of the phoenix rippled over his face. His eyes turned from honey to red and back again. "Don't."

I held my hands out and shrugged. "Don't what? I didn't do anything."

One little snogging session with her and he's got his knickers in a bunch. Girl must be magical in more than one way. I looked him up and down. "What's got your feathers ruffled?"

He surged forward and smacked both his hands on the wall beside my head. "One guess."

"Haven't the foggiest." With my vampire speed, I ducked under his arm and started walking out into the courtyard. "Hangry, perhaps? Did Polly forget to bring his crackers?"

"Grayson!" He shouted my name so loud I had to turn around.

"Yes?"

He reached into his pocket and then launched whatever it was at my face. Before it smacked into my eye, I lifted my hand and snagged the sharp metal from the air. They jingled in my hand when I turned to look at them. "Keys?"

"Yeah, you're driving." He stalked out into the courtyard and straight past me. The snow around him instantly melted away. He was throwing so much heat off his body. The continual flakes didn't even touch his head. Instead, they evaporated around him, sending little puffs of steam up into the air.

"Excellent."

I BELTED the "Chitty Chitty Bang Bang" song as loud as I could to break the silence in the small bus.

Nova sat directly behind me and had put her earbuds in a long time ago. But when I glanced into the rearview mirror, I saw Tucker in the back, his eyes glowing red and never wavering from my head. *Clearly, my plan is working. Perhaps too well.* Halfway back, Zinnia sat with her head resting on the cold glass, as she read from a thick book with a worn green cover. Her lips moved as she read. Within a few hours she was more than halfway through the tome. Magic shimmered in her hair and around her fingers, lighting up the pages. I didn't even think she realized she was doing it at this point. But when Tucker had ordered the others to give her a shot of their own magic, I knew instantly it was going to be too much. Only problem was how would it come out now?

When I went to check my mirror on the right side, Ashryn was bent so close to my face I flinched away. "What in the bloody hell are you doing?"

Her long sandy hair fell onto my shoulder, and her lilac scent filled my senses. The black puffy vest she wore over her long-sleeved white shirt rubbing against her leather pants was the only sound she made. "Grayson, I suggest you desist this wailing, or I will be forced to reach past your baby fangs and remove your tongue from your head. Thank you."

Ashryn stood up straight and walked back to her seat and sat down quietly with her back stiff and gaze forward. My jaw dropped open. The elf had barely said a word to anyone this whole time. Yet she took it upon herself to threaten me. *Not the person I expected that from.* Then suddenly, the mood in the small bus lightened, and they all broke out into fits of laughter. Even Tuck smirked. After a few hours of driving in silence, it was good to hear even a bit of laughter after what we'd been through earlier with Poseidon.

I winked at her in my mirror. "Right you are. I'll be sure to, how did you put it? Desist my wailing."

Ashryn was quietly beautiful with a small pert nose and high cheekbones. She was long and willowy. At times when she was around the other queens, it was easy to forget she was there. She was always so silent and calm. But when she gazed at me through the mirror with those forest-green eyes, there was wisdom. I didn't quite know where it came from.

"Yeah, Gray, I think you hit notes only werewolves would hear," Zinnia teased while she shoved her book into her backpack. Then she moved up closer to sit next to Nova behind me.

Nova plucked her earbuds out. "I couldn't even drown him out with my music."

"Brutal." Zinnia snickered.

Nova rolled her eyes. "Tell me about it."

I gazed out over the empty roads covered in snow. "Yeah, well, we are the only miserable gits driving in the mess, and I just thought a little music would do our morale some good."

Tucker rose from the back of the bus and sat in the bench seat opposite Nova and Zinnia. "Raise our morale by torturing us to your tone-deaf rantings. 'Chitty Chitty Bang Bang' my head up against a wall."

"Glad to see you're in higher spirits, boss. No one likes a silent parrot," I teased.

Tucker scoffed. "About as much as anyone likes a little leech stuck to their ear."

"Speak for yourself." Driving into Philly, I could see the snow-covered city. "But just to make you all feel better, I'll turn the radio on."

I flipped the switch and turned up the volume, expecting music to blare through the speakers on the bus. What I got was something else altogether. The DJ sounded exhausted as she read the news. "In other news, hundreds of thousands have been left without power as the storm continues. Measurements of well over six feet of snow have come up all across New Jersey and New York. The state water company encourages all of us to try to keep our homes as warm as possible to avoid pipes from bursting." Then I heard her slam the papers down on the desk. "Really? Try to keep the houses warm? We have no power, people, and the freak storm shows no sign of stopping. I haven't left the studio in forty-eight hours. Screw this." The station shut her down, and a slow song came back on.

I flicked the radio back off. "Well, that's enough of that. I do wonder something."

"Oh yeah?" Tucker leaned forward into the aisle, so close I could see him out of the corner of my eye.

"How are we driving and no one else can get through?" It was true while I drove I noticed the path ahead of us was clear, but on both sides of the bus, walls of snow rose up from the ground. There was no one else on the roads, not even emergency vehicles. The whole East Coast was buckled down for the duration.

Tucker nodded toward Zinnia. "Care to tell him what you've been doing?"

"I'll tell him what I've been doing if you tell him what *you've* been doing," she whispered back to him.

"Well, someone tell me, because we're almost there, and I need to know if we're going to get through or if we're hiking in six feet of snow. I, for one, would prefer not to do that." I turned off the highway, and again the bus was able to move through the snow.

Tucker chuckled. "I believe I've been melting, and Zinnia..."

"I've been removing with wind. Turns out Tabi's powers have come in handy."

I smirked. *Soul mates are stronger together.* "Well, I thank you for that." I wanted to scream *I told you so.* Instead, I kept my mouth shut as I made the last turn down Fairmont Street where the Eastern State Penitentiary stood.

Nova shot to her feet. "Stop!"

I slammed my foot down on the brake, and the bus slid forward on a sheet of ice. The back end flew straight up into the air, sending us tumbling. As we flipped upside down, I saw Tucker turn and brace his legs against the ceiling. Zinnia flew up from her seat, and he hooked his arm around her waist and caught her before her head smacked into the ceiling. Behind Nova, Ashryn twisted her body upside down and braced herself to hold Nova into the chair. The ceiling of the bus crunched and groaned as we skidded across the ice-packed snow. Glass shattered on all sides of the bus like it'd exploded from the outside in.

I leapt over the driver's seat and threw myself over Nova, covering her from the broken shards. The metal of the bus crumbled in on itself as it scraped against the street. The smell of gas smothered the air.

When the bus came to a stop, I held still. "Tucker?"

"I smell it," he whispered. "Everyone slowly move to the back door."

I took one step toward the emergency exit at the back when the engine wheezed and clicked. Then . . . *pop!*

We shot up off the ground in a ball of flames.

CHAPTER 21

ZINNIA

Flames spread up the sides of the bus and across the floor, which was the ceiling now that it was flipped upside down. The seats melted from the heat, and Tucker stood towering over me with his hands out to his sides, as if he was holding the bus up.

Sweat poured off him, and he gritted his teeth. "Everyone to the back door."

The flames peeled back from the door like a curtain. I looked up at Tuck. "Are you doing this?"

"Trying to. Combustible flames are more difficult to manage." His body shook from head to toe.

I reached out and grabbed Nova and Ashryn, then shoved them toward the door. "Everybody out. We don't have much time."

They scrambled to the back door. Ashryn stopped

and grabbed the metal lever to release the door but quickly jerked her hand back. She held her hand out to us. The skin across her palm was bright red and bubbling up. She hissed in a sharp breath. "Too hot."

"I've got this." I pushed past them and reached for the handle.

"Zinnia, don't—" Gray reached past me to grab the bar.

I shoved my shoulder into his side, knocking his hands away. "Don't touch it."

When I wrapped my hand around the handle, I felt how hot it was, but it didn't burn my hand. I opened up my magic and covered my palms in it, using every bit of it to protect my skin. Silver glittered over my skin, and I yanked the handle. Metal groaned against metal as the lock slid to the side. My pulse raced, and I took a step back, then lifted my leg and kicked the back door wide-open. Cool air rushed into the bus and blew my hair back from my face. I turned back and grabbed Nova's arm, yanking her toward the door. "Go now."

She tumbled out into the darkness, then I waved Ashryn forward. "You next."

"I'm sworn to protect you, my queen." She cradled her hand to her chest and stood still as stone.

I rolled my eyes and flicked my hand forward. Tendrils of my magic wrapped around her waist and legs like ropes. I yanked back, and her feet went out from under her as I tossed her through the door. I narrowed my eyes at Grayson. "You wanna give me a try?"

He held his hands out in surrender. "Not a chance." He darted past me.

Tuck stood in the center of the bus with his arms spread wide. His black T-shirt was sweat-soaked to his body. The muscles in his arms strained and shook as he struggled to hold the fire off. Billowing flames pressed against the invisible boarder he held in place. Black smoke seeped inside. "Go, I got this."

There was no way in hell I was leaving him behind. He may have been a phoenix, but every supernatural had their limits, and I didn't want to find out what his were.

I fisted both my hands in his shirt and yanked him to me. "Not a chance. We do this together."

He nodded, and his wings shot from his back. "Together."

"One . . ." I forced the elemental magic from my body. It brushed up against the wall he'd created with his own phoenix power. I could feel how close he was to losing his hold on it all. I knew I wasn't strong enough to hold it all on my own, but if we did it together, we might get an extra two seconds to get out. "Two . . ." I stepped in closer and pressed my chest to his and met his heated honey gaze.

"Three!" He wrapped his arms around my waist and pumped his wings, diving for the back door. I threw my hands around his neck and held on as we shot out like a bullet into the snowy light. The walls of magic we'd been using to hold the fire at bay dropped instantly, and the bus exploded up into the air, knocking us sideways. Tucker turned his shoulder and threw his back to the ground, breaking my fall. We skidded across the ground and smacked into a snow bank. Air whooshed from his lungs, and he sputtered and coughed.

I lay there for a moment, looking up into the pitch-black sky, watching the snow fall onto my face. The smell of burning rubber, gas, and Tucker's woodsy scent surrounded me. My head was cradled in the crook of his arm. I turned to my side to look down on him. "Are you okay?"

He pressed his eyes shut, and his brow furrowed as he groaned. "Yeah, I'm okay."

The snow around us crunched down with every step the others took toward us. Tucker coughed into his fist and rolled to face me. "Thanks."

Our noses were almost touching. If I titled my head only an inch forward, I would be able to press my lips to his. I wanted to do it. I wanted to celebrate the fact we survived an explosion in the best way. I didn't move. "Anytime."

His lips pulled up into a breathtaking smile. "You want to get blown up with me anytime?"

Heat flooded my cheeks. "That's not what I meant."

He reached up and wound his finger in a lock of my hair. "You are amazing, Zinnia Heart."

Grayson slid to a halt and hunched over us. "Bloody hell. Are you all right?"

Great timing. I rolled to my back and sat up slowly. Wet snow soaked into my jeans, and my skin instantly cooled. When I glanced to the side, I could see strands of my hair standing out from my head. *Lovely . . .* "Yeah, I think I'm okay."

"Me too." Tucker sat up. His face was covered in black soot and sweat. Flakes of snow clung to his dark hair.

"What happened?" I looked back at where the bus crumbled into a burning heap of nothing.

Nova came up behind Grayson. "It was the spirits." She stared at the ominous brick face of the prison. "They *liked* it."

A throbbing started in my head, and I pressed my hand to it. "They liked blowing us up? Why?"

"Because they can, Zin . . . because they can." Nova reached down and grabbed my hand, then hauled me to my feet. "We've got to get moving. I can feel them rushing toward us."

Tucker lumbered to his feet, then nodded toward the front of the prison. "Think this is the first time anyone has ever broken *into* a prison before?" He looked over his shoulder and then spun in a circle. "Where's Ash?"

Shit, did I throw her too hard? Panic sent my heart into my throat. I too spun in a circle, searching for her. When I looked up at the high brick walls, I spotted Ashryn tiptoeing across the top of it. She held her arms out as though walking on a tight rope. That wasn't the most amazing part of it all. On top of the wall, there was at least three feet of snow, which she didn't sink down into, not one bit. I raised my eyebrows and watched as she danced over it like a ballet dancer. Then she bent her knees and dove over the back side and out of sight.

I stumbled forward. "What's she doing?"

A sly smile cracked across Gray's lips. "My guess would be breaking and entering. She'll have the front door open in no time."

I nodded and took a step back. "If you say so."

The outside of the penitentiary was made of grayish brick that was covered in years of unkept filth. If I hadn't known what lay behind those walls, I might've thought it was a castle. Behind the outer wall stood a large tower with openings all around it. In the past, armed guards would've stood in that tower shooting down whomever even dared to leave.

I followed behind Grayson and Tucker as they made their way over to the huge double doors. When I glanced over my shoulder, I spotted Nova hanging back away from the rest of us. "Be right behind you."

I turned away from them and walked over to where Nova stood kicking at the snow on the ground. "Hey, what's up?"

She didn't meet my eye. Instead, she shook her head. Her pin-straight white blond hair fell over her face. "Nothing."

"Listen, Ashryn is about to open that door, and if you don't give me a heads-up what's wrong, I can't help you."

"You ever wonder why this is one of the most haunted places in the country?" When I shook my head, she met my eye. "It's because these spirits are so evil they know if they move on to the afterlife they'll be punished . . . so they stay here, torturing the living. The more aware someone is of their existence, the more they will act out."

"So, what you're saying is you're like a . . ."

"A freaking magnet to them all." She shook her head and sucked in a breath.

I turned and wrapped my arm around her shoulders.

"Remember that hit of magic Tuck made you give me before?"

She nodded. "Yeah."

"Well, I'll use it however you need me to. We just have to find the door to the underworld and get through it. Right?" I began walking and brought her with me.

"Right." She sighed.

Once we stood next to Tuck, he eyed her closely. "Everything all right?"

I dropped my arm from around Nova's shoulders and stepped up to the door. "Just fine. What's happening? Are we almost in?"

"Best be out of here before the authorities arrive to put that fire out." Grayson motioned to the bus.

"I think six feet of snow will be holding them up just a bit." When the locks on the other side of the door creaked open, I took a step back.

They swung open only a couple feet, then Ashryn popped her head out and waved us through. "Come on, let's go."

I followed Tuck through the door. When we were all on the other side, Ashryn shoved her shoulder into it and slammed it shut. Though this was now a tourist attraction, goose bumps broke out over my arms. I walked over to a shelf full of maps and plucked one up. "Here, let's figure out where we have to go. Nova?"

I opened it up and held it out for us all to see. Tucker snapped his finger, and that hanging flame he'd used in the closest only hours before appeared over the map. I sucked in a breath and locked gazes with him, wondering if he too was thinking about what'd happened. When a flush crept up his cheeks, I knew he was.

I shook my head, trying to focus on the task at hand. "Where do you think it is?"

The map showed the prison was broken up into six different wings and was in the shape of a huge asterisk. Grayson pointed to the titles of each of the wings. "I love the choices they've given us here: Lock Down, where they were left in their own mess; Quarantine, where they went insane; The Shop, where they used tools to kill each other I'm sure; The Infirmary, where they suffered to death; and the Blood Yard, which sounds like where they put them to riot. Right, and none of this is creepy at all."

Nova pressed both her hands to the sides of her head and paced back and forth. "It's in the Quarantine hall, all the way at the end."

My eyes widened. "How do you know?"

"Because . . . they're all talking to me."

CHAPTER 22

I crumpled the map in my hands and shoved it into my back pocket. "Come on, we gotta go."

I grabbed Nova's hand and ran through the lobby into the hallway that would lead farther into the prison. Tucker's flame lit the way ahead of us. The only problem was it only lit up about ten feet in front of us. Beyond that it was pitch blackness. The walls were crumbling in multiple places, with large chunks of white paint flaking off and falling. The sound of rattling chains echoed around the hall.

I skidded to a halt in a room that had six hallways shooting off of it. The room was domed with dilapidated wooden posts that where fractured in pieces. "What was that?"

"I don't know." Grayson raced to stand at the front of the pack. "But you two will stay behind me. Got it?"

I nodded. My pulse hammered in my chest, and I fought not to panic. Sweat covered my palms, and I knew Nova could feel it up against hers as I clung her hand tighter. But I couldn't let go of her, not now. Her skin was white as a sheet, and her dark eyes were as big as saucers. I shoved him forward. "Just remember we aren't vampires."

He nodded and took off down the hall on our right. We followed close behind him. It opened up to a narrow wing with two stories that were exposed down the middle and sectioned off by rusty railings. Dark doorways lined both floors, and a sliding rail hung above each one where the doors would've been to each cell. Though there were no door handles on them, the sound of sliding metal slamming and locking repeated over and over again.

I tugged on Nova's arm. "Where is it?"

"A-at the end of the hall." Her pace slowed, and I struggled to pull her along.

Tucker came up on her side and grabbed her other arm to help me move her forward. "What's wrong with her, Zin?"

My breaths came in panicked pants. "Sensory overload."

"What?" He swung his gaze around.

"The spirits are talking to her—"

Nova slammed her hands over her ears. "No, they're yelling at me."

"Go, go, go." I ran headlong. The hanging lights above surged from blinding bright to pitch-black. White dots swarmed my vision. With one hand I tugged Nova forward and with the other I rubbed my eyes. "We need to keep going."

Nova stopped dead in her tracks and sucked in a breath. "They're here."

Deep cackling echoed off the walls and up and down the hall. "I don't like this."

Tucker sent fireballs flying in front of us and behind us. Shadows swarmed and crawled over the walls and ceiling, heading in our direction, each one moving the way spiders and cockroaches do when the lights go on.

I grabbed onto the tops of Nova's arms and shook her. "What do we do to stop them?"

Tucker fired fireball after fireball at them. They just passed through the shadows without even bothering them. Ashryn drew her bow and held it up, but deep down I knew that wasn't going to help us.

Nova shook her head. "I don't know. There's too many of them."

"Then we keep going. We're almost there." I jerked my head toward the end of the hall.

Grayson turned. "Agreed." He took one step, then was lifted up off the ground and thrown back like a rag doll. His body twisted in the air, spinning toward us. He smacked into Nova and me, knocking us to the ground. I slammed into the cement floor with Gray's upper body pinning me down. The air left my lungs, and I struggled to suck in a deep breath. Suddenly, his body was thrown straight up into the air, disappearing into the darkness.

Tucker crouched down at my side. "We have to get ou—"

Tucker was thrown sideways and pinned to the wall with his arms and legs spread wide. Shadows froze over him, and his mouth disappeared, as if the skin had knit together. He looked at me with wide eyes. Ashryn was trapped to the opposite wall in the same position. When I stepped up to grab a hold of Tuck, the shadowy figures' heads all snapped toward me at once. I held my hands up and took a step back as they hissed at me with long teeth. Their beady glowing red eyes followed my every move.

I crouched down low next to Nova and whispered, "Nova, I need your help."

With her hands pressed to her ears, she sat on the ground, rocking back and forth. "They're showing me . .

. oh God." She squeezed her eyes shut. "They're showing me what they did to get in here. So many deaths, so much blood."

Then suddenly, she froze and tilted her head back. Her eyes shot wide-open. Her eyes were pure milky white. *Think, Zinnia, think!* I pressed the back of my hand to my mouth to stop the scream bubbling up my throat. I closed my eyes and held my hands out, tapping into the deepest part of me. I dropped down in front of Nova and crossed my legs. I wasn't sure why I thought sitting in a prison full of evil spirits was a good idea, but I had to help my crew. It was now or never.

I focused my gaze on Nova. "Nova, I know you can hear me. I need you to help me."

I grabbed her hands in mine and wound our fingers together. Purple sparks shot out of our joined hands. I didn't know what I was doing or how this was going to work. I'd been reading the book Professor Davis gave me. I couldn't recall a specific spell to help us here, but I had to try. I opened my magic up to everything around me and spoke the words that appeared in my mind. I summoned a flame with my mind and let it hover between Nova and me. When it started to smoke, I began to speak, "Through the flames of time and smoking desire, I call upon the higher power. Frozen in fear and lacking in sight, I bid you bring her back to rights."

Nova's eyes cleared of the milky white. She gasped and leaned in closer to me. I nodded to her, giving her the sign not to break my hold on her hands. *Halfway there, Zin.* "Sins of the past, fate of the present, let them freeze amongst their brethren. Frozen in time and bound by night, let them dwell forever out of sight. I bind thee all here and now, I bind thee all to your personal hell. The cells they call, they beckon thee. The cell will now be forever where you'll be!"

Purple sparks shot out from our bound hands, hitting every spirit in the chest. The shadowy figures strained against my spell. Their jagged hands reached out to me. Their mouths opened in high-pitched screams as they were sucked one by one back into the cells they'd spent their human lives in. Tucker dropped from the wall and landed in a crouch. Across from him, Ashryn landed lightly on her feet. Her hand flew up to her mouth, where she pressed her fingers over her lips.

"Aaaaaahhhhhhh." Grayson plummeted toward the ground. I held my hands out, trying to think of the spell I'd seen a teacher use on my first day at Evermore Academy. My mind went blank, and I felt exhaustion pulling me under.

Tucker thrust his wings from his back and leapt up

into the air, snagging Grayson around his chest. He landed only a foot away from me. Without a word, he dropped Gray at my feet.

He hit the floor with a thud but quickly sprang back up. His normal slicked-back hair was sticking out in wild tuffs around his face, and his eyes bulged out of his head. "What? What'd you say? I'm fine. Are you fine?" He pulled his sleeves up to his elbow. "Good, we're good. Let's go."

Grayson ran away, then came right back. He was so hopped-up on nervous energy that I suspected he could run a full marathon in minutes. He bounced on the balls of his feet. "By the way, where are they all? What did you do with them?"

I shrugged. "Sent them back to where prisoners belong. To their cells."

"Back to their cells for eternity. That's cold . . . but also so cool." When he began walking down the hall, I let my shoulders sag and sucked in a sigh. That spell was one of the hardest I'd ever done, and I couldn't help but wonder where the words had come from.

Tucker hooked his finger under my chin and lifted my face to meet his eyes. "You did amazing."

"Yeah, Zinnia. Thank you." Nova placed her hand on my shoulder for just a second before she walked past me.

Tucker winked at me, then jerked his head to point down the hall. "Shall we?"

I wanted to tell him I'd follow him wherever he went, but I was too tired to even speak.

"Oy, you lot, I think I've found it," Grayson called from the darkness.

I followed closely behind Tucker. My eyelids felt dry and heavy, almost ready to close at any moment. At the back of the hall was a small room with a single chair sitting in it. "I don't even want to know what this room is for."

Nova shook her head. "No, you really don't." When she looked at me, I could see the strain behind her eyes. She'd said the spirits showed her things. Part of me wanted to know exactly what she'd seen behind those milky white eyes, and the other part of me had seen enough of the inside of this prison to last me a lifetime. The moment she reached the back wall, she placed her hand on it and closed her eyes and whispered, "Open."

The wall fell away piece by piece, opening up into a black hole of nothing. Nova glanced over her shoulder. "No offense, but I want out of here." She stepped through and disappeared. Ashryn followed close behind her, followed by Gray.

Tucker stepped to the side and waved for me to go through. "You first."

As I passed by him, I felt the tips of his fingers brush over the back of my hand. "I'll see you on the other side." I took one step through the opening to the underworld, and the floor dropped out from under me.

My stomach shot up into my throat, and then I fell into an abyss.

CHAPTER 23

TUCKER

I woke with my face suctioned to some kind of horrible pink pool float. When I placed my hands up near my face and pushed off it, all the air shifted toward my legs and my face plummeted forward. The plastic creaked as I righted myself and returned to lying flat on my stomach. "What the hell happened?"

"Well, not hell exactly, but close enough," a deep, rumbling voice answered my question.

I clumsily rolled to the side and flopped onto the hard-packed dirt. I lay there for just a moment, looking toward the sky—only, there was no sky. I was in some kind of underground cave. Realization hit me, and I sprang to my feet. "Shit, I'm in the underworld."

"You would be correct." Again, that voice smoothly answered my question.

I whirled around and drew my swords. Flames exploded down my arms and all the way to the tips of my blades. "Where are they?"

"Easy there, kid." A man stood towering over me. He was at least six inches taller than I was, with black wavy hair that was combed back from his face. His violet eyes wavered from the darkest purple to the lightest pastel. A thick black goatee surrounded the large smile he was giving me. His skin held a summer tan, like he'd been lying on the beach for weeks. When he held his well-muscled arms out wide, I hesitated.

"Hades?" I didn't drop my swords. "God of the underworld?"

"Ah, well, we both know I'm not really a god . . . although . . ." He snapped his fingers, and four other chairs appeared next to the large plastic couch one I'd been lying on before. He motioned to the chairs. "Here are the rest of your friends."

There they all were peacefully sleeping, on an array of hideous furniture. "What's wrong with them?"

"What do you mean?" Hades tilted his head to the side and scanned them all.

Zinnia lay curled on her side across an old leather sofa with large cracks across the brown leather arms. On the top of the back, stuffing floated out of the tip, as if the couch had been chewed by a large dog. Her long black hair fell around her face and down her shoulder in a tangled mess. Beside her, Ashryn slept flat on her back on a bright red recliner. The chair tilted to the side as though broken in all different places. Nova was slumped over in a high-back wooden chair. How she sat like that, I didn't know, with her arms hanging limply at her sides and her head slumped down to her chest.

But the best of all, Grayson lay with his arms crossed over his chest like the dead . . . on a fluffy pink day bed, complete with lace pillows, a floral print comforter, and pink satin sheets. A wide smile spread across his face, and the tips of his fangs peeked out over his bottom lip.

I motioned to them. "I mean, why are they all still asleep?"

"Oh, well, that. I think it's exhaustion setting in. Tell me, are the rumors true? I hear you all survived a drowning and a fight with spirits. Seems like a lot." He shrugged and put his hands on his hips.

"Yeah, I guess." As I glanced around, I noticed we all stood on the side of a long dirt road that had no end and no beginning. In the distance, the sound of wailing echoed from pits that glowed like magma. Sheer rock faces rose up like mountains on every side. If we veered off the high path for even a moment, any one of us would fall into those. What was at the bottom of those pits?

"You don't want to know, kid. Trust me."

Did I just talk out loud?

"Yeah, you did, and it's getting kind of weird." Hades drew my attention back to my sleeping crew.

I shifted from one foot to the other, wanting to change the subject. "How do I wake them up?"

"Like this." He cupped his hands around his mouth and yelled, "Wake up!"

They all shot wide awake with a start. Zinnia slammed upright and threw her hand out. A stream of silver magic shot from her palm like a bullet straight at Hades' torso. He crossed his arms over his chest and took the hit head-on. It sent him skidding back at least thirty feet. He dug his feet into the ground. Dust and pebbles flew up around him, and a muscle in his jaw flexed as he gritted his teeth. Purple lightning forked out from his eyes. When he finally skidded to a halt, he started marching back with quick, determined steps.

Zinnia looked at her hand, as if it acted of its own accord. "Damn it." Her eyes flashed to mine. "I'm so sorry . . . I-I didn't know."

I rushed to step in front of her. I held my swords up, ready to fight him off. "Hades! You'll have to go through me."

Hades slowed his pace, then sucked in a deep breath

and straightened his stance to a trudge. "Don't worry, Phoenix, your girl is safe . . . for now."

CHAPTER 24

"Oh my God, I'm so sorry." The last thing I remembered was falling through the doorway to the underworld, then suddenly being startled awake.

"Again, not a god . . . Ah, what the hell." The man spread his arms out wide and smiled at me. "I am Hades, god of the underworld. And you are?"

God? I was under the impression they weren't gods, yet here he was calling himself a god. The air was oppressive, humid, and smelled of burning . . . like everything just burning. Though it was dim and cave-like, the walls glowed with veins of lava. When I gave it a closer look, I jumped back. Definitely not lava. There were faces amongst the flames, each of them crying out or reaching for something. Sweat began to run down my body, and I tried to focus on anything but the souls trapped down here. I felt as though it was the beginning of summer and I was dressed for the middle of winter.

I pulled my jacket off and tied it around my hips. "Um, I'm Zinnia."

He raised his eyebrows at me. "Ah, the notorious Siphon Witch." He gave a slight bow. "A pleasure to meet you."

Was this guy for real? This was not what I expected to encounter in the underworld. I expected more ghosts, zombies, maybe even some demons. But Hades of the Greeks, most definitely not.

I gave a tentative wave. "Nice to meet you."

"Right, okay." He clapped his hands together, then rubbed them back and forth. "Shall we go see some Furies about a man?"

Grayson sat up with a start and looked around, then held up a pink fluffy pillow with lace all around it. "What am I doing in a pink frilly bed?" He wrinkled his nose in disgust and tossed the pillow away. It landed off to the side, and a puff of dried dirt drifted up into the air.

Hades rocked back on his heels. "See, what had happened was, when you all fell into the underworld you landed hundreds of thousands of miles away from where you needed to be. I got a call from Taliam. He demanded that I find you and bring you to the Furies, or at least, that's what a woman named Niche was screaming in the background when I spoke to him. So here I am, your official tour guide of the underworld."

Tucker straightened his stance in front of me and extinguished his swords. "Still doesn't explain why we all passed out."

Hades shrugged. "What can I say? Time and space work differently down here. Or I could've put you all in a sleep trance and then summoned you all where you needed to be at the exact right moment to avoid days of this conversation with teenagers or you might've been tired . . . So are we going or not?"

When I glanced around, the road seemed pretty self-explanatory. There was only one direction to go in. To my right, it extended out into the distance, and to my left a couple hundred yards away, the road dead-ended into a sheer rock face. The walls all glowed molten red, and farther away, I heard torturous cries. But beyond that . . . *is that classical music?* The path seemed clear to me. It just rolled over barren hill after hill. Plus, I did not trust this guy. The last time we interacted with a Greek, the whole crew nearly drowned and froze to death. "I'm sure we can walk a dirty path on our own."

Just then, a loud screeching pierced the air. Puffs of dust rose up from the ground that rolled and moved like there was something underneath it. The pretty pink pillow Grayson had just tossed away was sucked down into the dirt. A moment later, cotton exploded from the hole like a geyser and an angry roar sounded.

Hades turned toward our group. "Excuse me for a moment, would you?"

He stomped his way out toward the middle of the barren hill. His long legs ate up the distance in four large strides. As he walked away from us, I noticed the small holes in his tight-knit V-neck sweater. He rolled his sleeves up to his elbows, then brushed his hands down his leather pants.

When he glanced over his shoulder at us, he held up his finger. "Just a sec."

He stood over the hole with his hands on his hips. A large serpent-like creature with arms too short for its twenty-foot-long body opened its mouth and flew at Hades' face. Fangs of a cobra flipped down from the roof of its mouth, dripping venom. It thrashed its head to the side and was about to bite his face when Hades' hand shot up and grabbed it by the neck just behind its wide-open jaw.

"Oh, you bad demon." He shook it violently. "Bad, bad, bad."

The demon hissed at him. Its body rolled and twisted like a snake. That's when I noticed its hind legs dangling down. Each of its feet had three long talons for toes. The serpent struggled against Hades' grip, then swung its leg out, aiming straight for his side.

I screamed, "Look out."

But Hades had already seen the move coming. He tossed the serpent high into the air, and when it came back down toward him, he pivoted on his heels and lifted his leg in a perfect roundhouse kick that connected with the creature's head and sent him flying into the great abyss. When he turned around to march back toward us, a large smile played on his lips and he dusted off his hands.

I took a step closer to Tuck. "What was that?"

Hades tilted his head back and laughed. "Demon. There are hundreds of thousands of them down here hunting for their next meal. You can see why Taliam would want me to help you navigate the underworld. It's no stroll in the park. But if you're content to do it alone, then I won't stop you."

When he turned to walk away, Tucker stepped up behind him. "I think we'd be grateful if you took us to the Furies. We only have four days to fix this mess, and if what you say is right about time being different down here, then I suspect that time is almost up." He glanced around at the rest of us. "Wouldn't we be grateful if he helped us?"

Without hesitation, I nodded. "Yes, very."

Hades rolled his eyes. "Fine. I'll take you, but I am not going in. Once you get there, you all are on your own. Those three don't like me."

I couldn't imagine why . . . cocky much?

CHAPTER 25

TUCKER

Never in my life did I think I'd be standing outside the den of Furies with two witch queens, a vampire, and an elf. It sounded like a bad joke waiting to happen. The steep rock face held two large metal double doors, each with depictions of three beautiful women carrying out acts of judgement. Sometimes they sat on thrones while people begged at their feet. Other times they carried out different forms of torture—or judgements, as they were called. Either way, we were about to walk into a den and a price would be paid . . . by whom, I didn't know.

Hades clapped me on the shoulder. "Good luck with them."

"Seriously? That's all you've got to say? Way to help out there." Frustration ran through me, and I didn't know which way to direct it. I'd almost died twice in one day, was put to sleep against my will, and I knew I couldn't keep up hiding things from Zin for much longer. She was my soul mate. I needed her, and she needed me . . . whether or not she knew it.

"Like I said, I was only told to get you here, not do it for you." He shrugged and took a step back.

The smell of delicious vanilla hit me a moment before Zinnia stepped beside me. "We faced the other challenges. We can do this too."

Her words sounded so confident, but deep down I felt her emotions, and I knew she was shaken. She'd barely had a week as a witch queen and here she was standing next to me about to walk into a den of Furies. Pride didn't even begin to describe what I was feeling for her, but it was the one emotion shining through the most right now. "Yeah, you're right, we can."

When I met her sapphire gaze, I felt her confidence in me. I didn't know what to do with that. All I knew was I was here to get something we needed to save the ice dragon and hopefully Zinnia's mother. I wanted to lean into her, press my lips to hers, and tell her *we've got this*. I was tired of hiding, tired of lying to her. Inside, it was slowly killing me to keep this from my soul mate.

Just when I was about to say screw it and kiss her,

Grayson walked up and wrapped his arm around her shoulder. "That's right, love. We've got this."

I fought the urge to rip his hand off. *He's on my team. He's on my team. He's on my team.* Jealousy seemed to be an emotion I was feeling every other second. It was foreign to me. I'd never felt this way before, but now standing here next to my soul mate, who was under another guy's arm, I couldn't even see straight. Gray lifted his other hand and knocked on the doors. Each rap of his knuckles sounded as though he were beating a drum in an empty cavern. The door creaked open only a sliver. When I peeked inside, I saw nothing but darkness.

Nova sighed. "Is anyone else thinking yay let's just step into the cave full of Furies and just see what happens?"

Ashryn actually chuckled. I'd never heard her laugh before, but there it was. In the middle of the under-world, about to enter a den full of Furies, and her tinkering laugh pierced the eerie silence.

She pressed her hand to her mouth. "Excuse me."

My lips pulled up into a smile, and then a chuckle burst from my chest. There wasn't anything funny about what we were going to do. Perhaps we were cracking up because of the mission, the pressure and nearly dying. Or perhaps we were long overdue for a break in the tension. Then Zinnia ducked out from under Gray's arm and hunched over and started laughing too.

"You're all bloody daft in the head, you are." Gray shoved his shoulder into the door and forced it open wider. "Come on then. Why are we standing here laughing when we've got things to do?"

I pressed my lips together, trying not to chuckle anymore, even though my shoulders still shook. The tension had to be broken somehow, but who would've thought it would be the Queen of Death and the somber elf? "Okay Gray, you're right. Let's get going."

When Zinnia stepped behind him and in front of me, I almost sniggered again. She was stuck between two guys but didn't even know it. I summoned my swords back to my hands and lit them up. "Weapons at the ready," I warned the others. I heard Zinnia groan and immediately knew she was thinking about how she'd cut down the punching bags with her blades.

"Pst, Zin."

"Yeah?" she whispered back without turning around.

"Did you bring your blades?" As we passed through the door, I moved up beside her. When she shook her head, her wild hair fell around her heart-shaped face.

"Open your hand." I'd never manifested a blade for anyone else before or tried to put one in someone else's hand. But I didn't want her to be unarmed in this situation. We didn't know what we were walking into. I closed my eyes for a second, visualizing the round blade that was connected by a handle on each side, with a phoenix on one side and the queen's half-moon mark on the other. The half-moon matched the one on her shoulder, the one that was burned into my memory since the first night I'd met her.

When she gasped, I opened my eyes and held my sword to light her palms. There sat the two perfect blades I'd envisioned just for her. "Use them well."

A smile tugged at her lips as she wrapped her fingers around the leather-bound hilts. "Oh, I will."

The flapping of wings drew my attention upward. In the darkness, I couldn't see anything, but gusts of wind brushed against my face, sending my hair flying back. When I lived among the phoenix, I'd grown used to this kind of interaction with others. But standing here about to take on a Fury, I wasn't so comfortable knowing they were flying over us, waiting to swoop down at any moment.

A high-pitched cackling broke the silence. "Oh, Phoenix, how you interest me."

Torches burst to life one by one in sequence down the sidewalls. At the back of the room, a line of fire sparked to life and surrounded a stage high up off the ground. Large stone steps led to the stage where three thrones sat empty. The thrones were made of ornate gold, and red velvet cushions lay on the seat of each of them. The flames surrounding the stage were so bright the heat licked at my face.

A woman with large black bat-like wings dropped down from the ceiling. Scraps of red gauzy material crisscrossed over her chest, leaving her flat stomach completely exposed. The skirt, if you could call it that, was made of strips of the same red gauzy material. It hung low on her waist and had long slits that ran up each of her thighs. Dark brown hair was piled high on top of her head in a mess of curls. She made a show of looking me over with her heavily lined cat-like eyes. "What brings you here, Phoenix?"

She climbed over the armrest of the throne in the center of the three. Her bat wings hung over the sides and scratched against the floor. Two other women landed just beside their thrones. They were dressed similar to the first one who'd landed, except one had long straight red hair, and the other had long blond hair that was braided down the side of her body. Each of them moved like wild creatures. They tilted their heads the way birds did but moved like felines. Each time the one in the middle gazed at me, I felt like someone was poking me from the inside out.

I stepped forward. How did one address a Fury? "Madam Fury, I have come—"

She threw her head back and cackled. "I am Megaera. You may call me Megaera." She pointed to the redhead on her left. "This is my sister Alecto." Then she pointed to the blonde on her right. "And this is my other sister Tisiphone. Why have you come to see us, Phoenix? It's not often that we host witch queens." She inclined her head toward Zinnia and Nova. "Or vampires." She spat the word *vampire* as though it were a curse. "Or children of the earth, or even shifters. Your presence here intrigues me."

Zinnia stepped forward and bowed. "Megaera, we come on urgent business. Alataris—"

Tisiphone turned her head away and started to scream while ripping at her blond braid. When she shot to her feet, I wanted to raise my swords to ward her off. But she changed directions so quickly and walked over to a large metal candelabra that stood six feet tall. She plucked it up off the ground, then bent the stand like a pretzel. She hoisted it over her head and threw it against one of the cave walls. It dented the hard rock and fell to the ground. She sucked in a huffed breath, then marched back to her throne, where she resumed her seat as if nothing had happened. "You were saying?"

Zinnia stared at her with wide eyes, and her mouth

dropped open. I gently elbowed her side, getting her attention. When she snapped her mouth shut, she paused for a moment. "Yes, he seems to have that effect on people."

Tisiphone nodded and examined her nails. "Indeed, he does."

I cleared my throat. "We believe Alataris"—Tisiphone tensed and opened her mouth to scream again. I rushed my words out before she could—"left something of great value in your keeping, and we need it."

Megaera sat forward and rested her chin on the back of her hand. "Interesting, and pray tell me why should we give you what you want? That is, if we even have it."

Back at the library, Niche was sure they had the map that would lead us to Alataris' safe where we believed the dragon heart scale was kept. Now standing here before the Furies, I knew they had it. In my gut, I felt it was here. "Our research shows this will be the best possible place he would've hidden it."

Megaera slouched back in her chair. "What is it you seek, exactly?"

"A map, leading to Al—" Zinnia cut off his name at the killing look Tisiphone gave her. "*His* hiding place. A vault to be exact."

"And what would you give for this *map*?" Megaera

smiled down at us, and I saw a gleam in her eyes. The gleam of mischief...

Zinnia pursed her lips. "What are you asking for?"

Megaera crossed her legs. "Come now, Zinnia, Siphon Queen, if we are to enter into a negotiation, you must name your terms."

When Zin turned and looked at me for help, I sighed, knowing this would not go well. "We would owe you a debt to be paid at any time in the future."

"Did you really just offer us an I.O.U.?" Megaera's shoulders bounced as she chuckled and glanced around at her sisters. "Oh, Tucker Brand, Prince of the Phoenix Clan, I think we can do better than that, don't you?"

"Prince?" Zinnia whispered, almost to herself.

"You didn't know?" Megaera stood and began walking down from the stage. Her hips swayed with each step she took. Her hair bounced and glistened in the firelight. The gauzy material of her dress floated around her as though a fan were blowing. The spark in her eyes made me want to take a step back. She clicked her tongue at me and shook her head. "Such secrets and lies, Phoenix. I do wonder—"

"A favor from the witch court should not be taken lightly," I interrupted her. But how could I not? My heart raced in my chest. There were so many things I wanted to tell Zinnia but hadn't. If everything I'd been keeping from her came out now, would she forgive me? Or even better yet, would she trust me ever again? No, it couldn't come out now. I would tell her at the right time. A time when we were alone, and I could explain myself. But not here and not now.

The flames all around the room shot high and flared. Megaera raised her eyebrows at me. "You dare interrupt me? You, who are but a mere blip in my extensive life-time." She waved her hand in my direction. "Be off with you. I've grown bored with this."

Zinnia stepped past me to meet Megaera halfway up the stairs. "Too bad we didn't come here to entertain you."

"Zinnia." When she glanced at me over her shoulder, I motioned for her to come off the stairs. "Don't."

She turned back to face Megaera. "In case you haven't noticed, Alataris . . ." She narrowed her eyes at Tisiphone. "Save your screaming. You're clearly the one he nailed and bailed. Which makes me wonder, why is she deciding who you give the map to?" Then she turned back toward Megaera and met the Fury's eyes head-on. "You haven't even named your terms, and you're dismissing us while he is freezing half of America? And what happens to you when Karroust is released? Hmm, have you thought of that? What would a giant of the seas do to three Furies responsible for punishing people? I mean, who even put him in there as his punishment to begin with?"

Megaera lifted her chin high into the air. "Who told you it was us who chose his punishment? It could've been the fates."

"It could have. But when Karroust gets free—and if you don't give us that map, I know he will—I'll be sure to let him know my opinion on who it was who decided to encase him in ice for all eternity. I guess he'll be more than understanding. I mean, with those red scars all over his body and that sword that's the size of, well, a tree." Zinnia made a fake gagging sound. "He definitely won't have anything to do with you guys at all."

Megaera bent down low, getting very close to Zinnia's face. I squeezed the swords in my hands, ready to take action if I need to. Zinnia twisted the blades in her palms as well. The Fury spoke through thinned lips, "Are you threatening me?"

"I wouldn't dream of threatening you. Ever." Zinnia leaned in a little closer. "I'm only asking what your price is for that map."

"Little witch is a tricky bit—"

"I wouldn't finish that sentence if I were you." I moved closer to Zinnia, ready to fight.

Megaera extended her wings out wide and launched herself backward to land on her throne. "The arrogance you both have shown is utterly distasteful to me." She waved her hand away as though bored with the two of us.

I grabbed Zinnia's arm and turned her away. "Come on, they're not going to help us."

As we began stomping down the stairs, Megaera called out, "There is one thing . . ."

"Name it." I looked at her over my shoulder.

"I desire a glimpse."

I spun on my heels to face her. "A glimpse of what, exactly?"

A wide smile spread across her lips. "A glimpse into your mind, young prince. A glimpse of the present will tell me much of the future."

Grayson tsked. "You can't be serious. A map to look into his mind? Seems a steep price to pay, love."

"I'll do it." We didn't have time to sit here and play games or wait for them to be gracious. We needed the map now. We needed to find the dragon scale and free the ice dragon before the giant broke free, before Alataris turned the whole eastern seaboard into the next Antarctica. All because he wanted vengeance against us for protecting Hexia.

"Wise decision." She rose up from her throne and expanded her bat wings to their full length. With one flick of her wings, she was shooting at me. Her sisters followed close behind her, all three of them swooping in.

Zinnia leapt to my side. "No!"

"Let them." I pushed her into Gray's arms.

She titled sideways and fell into him. "What?"

"Let them!" It was the last two words I spoke before Megaera smacked into me and lifted me up off the ground.

My back slammed into the hard rock face. Jagged edges poked into my skin. Pain shot through my body. Below me, I heard Zinnia screaming my name, but I couldn't see her. We were too high up. Megaera's hand was pressed to my neck. I gasped for air. My vision was full of their faces. They all swirled together. Megaera brought her long nail under my chin, forcing me to meet her gaze. "Hold still, young prince. This won't take long."

A viper wound down her arm, slithering toward my face. Its fangs dripped with venom as it opened its jaw wide.

I turned my head away. "This wasn't part of the deal."

"A peek for the map." Megaera gave me a cold smile a moment before the snake struck.

Its fangs sank into my cheek, and the muscles from my face all the way down to my toes went limp. My body slumped back against the wall, and I was suddenly drowning in my memories. Visions of my mother and her hot cocoa scent swirled together with my punishing training sessions with Blackwing and the first time I'd faced him as a fully-changed phoenix. All the pain of the trials surged through my body as though I was reliving them. And then suddenly, it all stopped, and there she was like a shining light in the darkness . . . Zinnia. I focused on her bright face. The Furies melted away to nothing. Everything was gone, and I felt as though I was floating. Pictures of all the times she'd caught my eye flashed through my mind, and then a clear vision of the thick band around my wrist that matched the thin band around hers perfectly.

"Ah, and that is exactly what I am looking for." Megaera's voice felt like it came from so far away. "Well done, young prince. Our bargain is struck. Your secret is safe with me . . . for now."

CHAPTER 26

I wanted to climb up the wall after Tucker. Though it was only minutes since he'd been taken, it felt like hours. He'd disappeared out of the reach of the firelight into the darkness above. His muffled bellows were cut off suddenly, and then there was utter silence. I was terrified for him. I glanced down at the blade in my hand, wondering if I should throw it.

Grayson followed my gaze. "I wouldn't if I were you."

"I know. I could hit him."

Ashryn came to stand at my other side. "Yes, but if you cut a Fury, the consequences would be . . . steep."

"Yeah, like under penalty of death." Nova joined us, completing the circle. "We just have to wait."

My body spun toward the door of its own accord. "What is happening?" The others were all moving like robots as we each fought not to be pushed out the door. Yet my legs kept on walking like the march of a wooden soldier. As I was about to go back out the door we came through, I grabbed onto the doorjamb and tried to hold myself in the den of Furies. Tucker hadn't returned, and I was not leaving without him. Nova was the first to be forced out, then Ashryn.

Grayson held on to the other side of the doorway. "I think we've been asked to leave."

My legs were flailing wildly, but I still held on. My back slammed into the ground, and I felt like I was being dragged out. I clung to the doorjamb by the tips of my fingers. "I'm not leaving without Tucker."

One of my hands slipped free. I gritted my teeth. Why would they kick us out this way? What were they doing to him? The thought of Tucker being trapped with those three *women* made my skin crawl. Not to mention the constant worry I'd been feeling since he left my sight. We'd spent the past few days in constant contact, and now I hated not having him with me. When my other hand slipped free, it was like my body went on autopilot and I shot to my feet. My arms and legs stiffly speed walked me right out the door and back to where we'd left Hades.

I abruptly stopped short just in front of Hades. "What just happened?"

He shrugged. "My guess is the Furies were done with you."

I spun on my heels and marched back toward the large double doors. When I smacked into an invisible barrier, a scream of frustration bubbled up my throat. "How do I get back in?"

"You don't."

I jabbed a finger at Hades. "That is not an answer. You're Hades. Get me back in there."

"I don't think you want back into the Fury den. Especially once they've expelled you out." He moved to the side and waved to a new set of five more hideous chairs, each one more broken down than the other. "Now, which one do you hate the most?"

"Ugh! What is it with you and these stupid chairs?" I threw my hands up. "Tuck is still in there, and either you help me get him back or so help me I will level that whole place."

I gathered my magic around me, letting it swirl up my legs around my body and down my arms. The ground began to shake, and I relished the feel of it. A long crack opened from where I stood all the way back to the doors to the Fury den at least a hundred yards away.

Nova wrapped her hand around my wrist. "Zinnia, stop!"

"Why?" My hair blew back away from my face.

"Shouldn't Tabi's powers have drained out of her by now?" Nova turned toward Ashryn. "Shouldn't they have?"

Ashryn nodded. "Yes."

I didn't feel them leaving me any time soon. I knocked away Nova's grip and raised my hands over my head, about to open that crack even wider.

Hades jumped in front of me and grabbed my wrists. "I wouldn't do that."

"Too bad I don't care." Tucker was trapped in there, and I'd do whatever it took to get him back. He might not feel the same way about me as I did about him, but I didn't care. I wanted him back, and I wanted him back now! Silver streams of my magic floated from my fingers. A brown scroll appeared in my grasp, quelling my magic for a second.

Hades took a step back. "Looks like your boy held up his end of the bargain."

I lowered my arms and held the paper close to my chest. "Then where is he?"

The doors to the Fury den creaked open, and Tucker strode out toward us. I'd never seen him so worn. He didn't hold his head up with his shoulders back the way he normally did. He trudged toward us with his head hanging low and his shoulders hunched forward.

Strands of his dark hair fell into his eyes, and his lips were pressed into a hard line. When he stood in front of me, he didn't give me that cocky grin I'd grown so attached to. His eyes were laser-focused on the rolled-up paper in my hand. "Did you get it?"

I held it up. "Yeah, I think so."

"You think so?" He reached out and plucked it from my hands. "Let's check, shall we?"

"Are you okay? What happened in there?" When I placed my hand on his arm, he stiffened and looked at it as if it would burn him.

"Nothing, I'm fine." His cold demeanor sent a clear message . . . he wasn't talking about it.

Yeah, we'll be talking about it later. For now, I let him turn our focus toward the map. When he unfurled it, there were three spots marked on it with golden symbols. One was a small key, one was a lock, and one was just a dot that jumped all over the place. I sucked in a breath . . . *Mom.* I poked a finger on the moving spot. "That has to be the island."

Tucker nodded. "I think so."

Grayson leaned over my shoulder. "What's that there? A key?"

"It'd make sense for the vault to have a key." Tucker pointed to another spot on the map. "So, we have to go here first."

I wanted to go after my mother right way, but then we'd lose the element of surprise. If we were going to free the dragon, then we could get her at the same time. Patience was not one of my virtues, but for her, I would make sure I was more than ready. Because when it came to rescuing her, there would be no second chances.

I grabbed the corner of the map and squinted at the glowing key symbol. "Is that in Seattle?"

Hades grabbed the map from Tucker's hand and sighed. "It's the Space Needle, to be exact. Damn it."

"Why damn it?" I didn't want him to have his hands on that paper any longer than necessary. I reached out and gently took it from him, then folded it and gave it back to Tuck, where I knew it'd be safe.

"Because the Space Needle isn't just a building. It's a combination lock, which means the people who I thought owned it have been evicted without knowing it, and now Alataris has taken it for his own." Hades stabbed his hands in his hair. "Matteaus is going to be pissed."

"But why?" I had to know what we were up against and who else would be involved.

"Never you mind that, you all have to get to Seattle and get that key." Hades placed two fingers in his mouth and gave a loud whistle.

"But we don't even know where to look for it. It

could be anywhere in the Space Needle." The ground began to shake once more, and it sounded like a stampede was heading right toward us.

"The top of it is a combination. Figure that out and you'll get the key." He turned his back toward us and put his hands on his hips as though he was waiting for something.

I grabbed Tucker's arm. "We don't even know how we're going to get there." The ground shook so hard I had to hold my other arm out to keep my balance. "We need to get out of here before whatever that is gets here."

Hades called over his shoulder. "You said you were going to need a ride. Well, I've got one for you."

A dog the size of a Mack truck thundered into view, only this one had three large heads. Its fur was so black it'd be impossible to see at night. Drool dripped from each of its mouths and fell to the ground in sticky puddles.

I took a small step back and shook my head. "You want me to ride that thing to Seattle?"

The dog towered over Hades by at least two stories. Its teeth had to be the size of trees. Yet when Hades held his hand up, the dog flipped over onto its back. Its tongues hung out of the side of its mouths. When he wagged his tail, the ground rumbled with a *thump, thump, thump.*

"He's not a thing." Hades climbed up onto its stomach and used his whole body to scratch it. "He's a good boy, isn't he?"

The dog's back leg kicked back and forth like Hades was hitting the right spot. As he wriggled over the ground, dirt and dust floated off the ground and billowed out toward us. This wasn't a guardian to the gates of the underworld, this was a way overgrown puppy.

I hesitated. "Tuck, I don't know if I can do this."

Hades jumped down and landed right in front of me. "You said you all need to get to Seattle quickly. Well, the underworld has tunnels all over the world. Cerberus here knows them all."

The middle head was panting so hard I was enveloped in hot dog breath so strong it blew my hair from my face. Behind Hades, the head on the right drooled a wad of slobber the size of a boulder. It fell to the ground with a squishy sound. I barely stopped myself from gagging.

Tucker sighed. "I don't see any other way."

Hades clapped his hands together. "That's right, everyone up."

Well, crap . . .

CHAPTER 27

I stood behind Zinnia and placed my hands on her hips. When she leaned back into me, I couldn't help but wonder when the Furies were going to use my secrets against me or the rest of the queens. It could break the whole crew apart, and they needed me. She needed me.

Zinnia brushed her hair over her shoulder and looked up at me with those dazzling sapphire eyes. "I'm not ready for this."

"You are." She was the strongest girl I'd ever known. I lifted her up over my head and placed her on the back of Cerberus' right head. "Make sure you hold on to the collar, okay?"

She swallowed, then nodded. I didn't want to leave her side, but I had to make sure Nova was loaded up on the left head of Cerberus. I took one step toward her, and a large tongue ran up my back. *Ugh, perfect.* My hair had to be standing on end, and the back of my jacket felt soaked. I didn't dare take a whiff of myself. After being tossed around in the underworld and given a tongue bath by a three-headed dog there was no way I smelled good. I lifted my hand and ran my fingers under the chin of the middle head, where Ashryn was already on board and ready to go.

I gave her a thumbs-up. "Are you good to go?"

She reached forward and patted Cerberus on the head. "This creature is wonderful."

"Yeah, well, you're driving, so don't steer us wrong."

She pressed her hand to her chest. "I would never."

I patted Cerberus just under his ear. The strands of his fur were as long as my arm. "Good."

I strolled over to where Grayson was about to help Nova up. He held his hands out in front of him. "Up you go, Nova."

Without hesitation, she placed her foot in Grayson's waiting hands and stepped up as if she was mounting a horse. She threw her leg over and settled herself in behind the dog's big, floppy ears. For the first time this whole trip, a wide smile spread across her face.

I leaned up against Cerberus' side. The soft fur tickled the back of my neck and arms. "You all set?"

"More than ready. This is so cool." She laced her fingers around one of the threads of the collar.

When I turned to head back toward Zinnia, I found Grayson walking over to her. Enough was enough of this. I strode after him. There was no way he was going to ride with Zinnia. As he reached up about to hoist himself behind her, I grabbed onto his arm and pulled him back down. "You can ride with Nova."

His lips tilted up in a half smirk. "Is that so?"

"That is so." I crossed my arms over my chest, remaining unmoved. If he wanted to challenge me over this, then *bring it on, baby leech.* I was getting close to drawing a line in the sand. If he wanted to try to cross it, then so be it.

"You sure you want to?" He glanced at Zinnia. "I really don't mind, you know? She's quite fit."

I curled my hands into fists. *She's quite fit? I'm not going to hit him. I'm not going to hit him.* For years, I'd worked on keeping my emotions hidden. This would be no different. "I'm sure."

Grayson shrugged, then patted me on the shoulder. "Just remember hands to yourself, mate."

Is he for real? "Just remember it's none of your business where my hands go." I squatted low, then jumped up and landed right behind Zinnia.

"Whoa!" She startled and her body began to slowly slide to the side. "Oh no. Whoa, whoa, whoa."

Before she could slide all the way off, I reached out and grabbed her arm, pulling her upright. Her back pressed in my chest, and her long hair tickled over my cheek. "Thanks."

Her breaths came in panicked puffs. I leaned in close to her ear. "Don't worry. I've got you."

When I wound my arms around her waist, she let her hands rest on my forearms. She pressed her fingers into my skin. "Don't let me go."

"Never." Though she probably suspected I meant while we rode this big ass dog, I meant it for so much longer after that.

Hades strolled out in front of us. "He knows where he's going. Just hold on. If you fall off, well, I've already fulfilled my duties to the Fallen, so you are on your own, my friends." He gave us a mocking salute, then disappeared into thin air.

Cerberus took off like a jet. Zinnia's whole body pressed against me. Her back melted to my chest, her thighs rubbed mine, and her warm vanilla scent surrounded me. We were moving so quickly my hair blew back from my face. This close to her, I couldn't stop myself from brushing her hair from her neck and running my fingers down her cheek. She leaned into my touch. I wanted it to be like this always. With her by my side. But if anyone found out about us being soul mates, it could all end in the blink of an eye. When she rested her hand on my thigh, my heart leapt up into my chest and I could barely breathe. I held still. I just wanted it to last a bit longer.

"Woohoo!" Grayson whooped from the other side of the dog, drawing me back to the present.

"Nearly there." Ashryn leaned her body to the side, and Cerberus turned and ran down a long tunnel. *Nearly there? No, not yet!* I'd only had a moment with her this close to me. Up ahead, there was a pinprick of light that seemed to grow bigger and bigger each second. Cerberus yelped and jumped like a puppy. His tail smacked the walls of the tunnel each time he wagged it. Drops of drool flew back from his oversized jowls. Each one splattered over the ground and walls with a sickly sounding splat.

The light at the end of the tunnel grew so big I knew my few moments with Zinnia were nearly over. I knew the others couldn't see us, so I wrapped my arm around her waist and hugged her closer. My heart raced in my chest from having her this close to me. Cerberus skidding to a halt sounded like the nails on his paws were grinding against hardwood floors. I dropped my hand away from her and instantly regretted the distance between us as I slid off to the side.

From on top of Cerberus, she looked down at me with a bright smile. Her sapphire eyes danced with excitement, and she looked every bit the queen she was. "Well, that was . . . interesting."

"Wasn't it?" I lifted my hand up, offering it to her.

Zinnia kicked her leg over and slid down the side of Cerberus into my waiting arms. "Are we here?"

Grayson ran to her side and lifted her out of my arms then spun her around. "Wasn't that fun?" His windblown hair fanned out around his eyes, making them look even wider with exhilaration.

"Um, yeah, it was." She tucked a lock of her hair behind her ear. As Grayson wrapped his arm around her shoulder and guided her out toward the opening of the tunnel, Zinnia hesitated only a moment, then went along with him.

I gritted my teeth. How could there still be something between them? Were they just friends, or were they more? The jealousy and curiosity was killing me. Part of me knew Gray was a great guy. The other part of me didn't give a crap. I wanted to yank his arm away from her. I wanted to stop them from being together. But I had a destiny to fulfill, and if I did my job the right way, she and I could be together . . . if she still wanted me by then.

Frustration bubbled up inside of me, and I curled my hands into fists. How much more of this could I take? I couldn't look at the two of them anymore. I spun on my heels and walked over to Nova, hoping for a distraction from them. "Are you okay?"

"I'm great. I love dogs." I'd never seen Nova so animated before. Usually she was quiet, somber even. She stretched her arms high above her head and scratched under Cerberus' neck. He belly flopped down in front of her with a loud thud. The ground quaked under my feet, and he rolled over onto his back with his many tongues hanging out the sides of his mouths. And I swear those three heads were smiling as she continued to pet him.

Nova giggled. She actually giggled. "Good puppy."

Good puppy? "Come on, Nova. We've got to get going." I motioned toward the end of the tunnel. I didn't want to end her time with Cerberus or ruin what little fun she was having, but we had to get to the Space Needle, and we had to get there soon. I waved for her to follow me, but when I turned, I was once again following behind Zinnia and Grayson. Ashryn filed in beside me. I had Nova on one side and Ash on the other.

Nova glanced over her shoulder and waved. "Bye, puppy!"

In answer, Cerberus yelped and wagged his tail, again knocking against the walls and sending dust and rocks raining down behind us. As we approached the small opening of the tunnel, the wall shifted and spun wide-open to accommodate us walking through. We came out just under the Space Needle. We'd stepped through an opening in a wall, but when we came out on the other side, the world twisted and we were suddenly standing above the opening to the underworld, like it was a manhole in the middle of the street. I bent over the hole and watched Cerberus flip back to his feet and trot off in the opposite direction. "Thanks, bud!"

The resounding bark that came out of the hole before it spun and closed up told me he'd heard me. A smile tugged at my lips. *The guys will never believe we rode Cerberus!* No matter how hard this mission has been I'd seen some things I'd never dreamed of. Even now I stood in a city I never thought I'd see under a landmark I'd only read about in books. A small thrill went through me as I turned to look up at the Space Needle.

Three sloping legs held the saucer-shaped building high in the sky, and a needle stood straight up, reaching for the stars. The sun had just begun to set, and I knew we'd have to wait until the Needle closed to visitors to be able to open the combination lock and get the key out. The five of us stood side by side, gazing at our next mission. What lay in wait for us, I didn't know.

My cell that'd been silent since we'd been in the prison went haywire, vibrating like mad in my pocket with unanswered messages. I shoved my hand in my jeans and pulled it out.

Beckett:

Where are you?

Things aren't good here

You better not be dead, or I'll kill you

Call me

Call me now

Fighting a losing battle. Hope you're doing better.

I hit the keys in quick succession: *In Seattle going to see about a key. Hold on just a bit longer.*

Then his text came back through. *We don't have much longer.*

To punctuate his words, the skies opened up and sheets of rain fell down on us, soaking me clear through. I shoved my phone back in my pocket and strode toward the entrance to the Space Needle. "Come on. We haven't got much time."

CHAPTER 28

I*'m in a closet . . . again.* Tucker stood so close to me that each time I took a breath his warm, woodsy scent mixed with cleaning supplies was all I could smell. Heat drifted off his body, warming the small room to a steamy degree. Standing this close to him, my clothes were nearly dried. Though he was hot as could be, he was treating me with a coolness I didn't like. The more attention Gray showed to me, the angrier Tucker grew. Since the beginning, I knew there was something between us, but now standing here with him, I had to wonder if he was my soul mate. Grayson said soul mates were traditionally within the same species. I was a witch, and Tuck was a shifter. Did that mean we weren't a traditional couple? Or did it mean my soul mate was someone else?

"I can't believe you," he hissed under his breath.

"Me?" I pressed my hand to my chest. "What did I do?"

"Nothing."

I was glad the others had to take up other hiding places in the Needle. It was the first time he and I had been alone since arriving at the prison. That seemed like a lifetime ago. "You might as well say it."

"Do you think it wise to flaunt your relationship with Grayson? Niche made it perfectly clear there was to be no fraternizing between all of us. It's safer that way." The only light in the closet was coming from the cracks around the door. Even so, it was enough for me to see the hard planes of his face were turned down into a scowl.

"Not that it's any of your business, but Grayson and I aren't in a relationship." I curled my hands into fists at my side.

"Psh, could've fooled me."

"What's it to you? Are you jealous? Or are you just that bossy?" Either way, he was pissing me off with his mood swings. *He likes me, he doesn't. He's jealous, he's not.* A girl could get whiplash from him.

"No." He pressed his lips together.

Always with the short answers. They were no answer at

all. "You know what? I'm fed up with this." I shoved the door wide-open and walked out.

"Zinnia, don't." He grabbed my arm and pulled me back in. "We need to wait just a bit longer to make sure no one is left here."

"Tucker, it's been quiet for two hours. I think we're good."

"Oy, you lot. Let's get a move on. We haven't got all night," Grayson called from the other side of the door.

"I couldn't agree more," I mumbled and pushed through the closet door. The inside of the Space Needle was surprisingly high-class. I'd expected just a blank viewing room to look out the windows. What I got was something else. Table and chairs were placed around the whole room, with thick dark furniture and plush carpets in a high-end restaurant. Closer to the windows, there was a room for people to stand and take in the view. High above Seattle this late at night, all I could see were the pinpricks of light from the city below.

Tucker marched out past me. "Since we've all decided to go." He glanced over his shoulder at me. "I guess we're going."

I wanted to stick my tongue out at him. In truth, I barely resisted the urge. But I stopped myself and followed in his wake. The tension between us was so thick I could chop it with an axe. How much longer could we go on like this? Each time we were close it was electric between us. I was aware of his every move and each time I looked at him he seemed to be right there. It was too much and not enough all at the same time. It was getting more and more difficult to focus on the mission at hand. We were getting close to a breaking point, but I didn't know which way we'd go. *Head in the game, Zin. Head in the game.* I shook myself and turned to focus on navigating our way through this and finding the key.

At the center of the Needle was a bank of elevators, and a little past that was a service stairwell. Tucker grabbed the handle and jammed his shoulder into the door. The metal groaned and scraped open. Before us was the service stairwell with its concrete walls and steps, with a metal handrail running along them. The railings were the round gray ones that seemed to be universal in every building I'd ever been in. The walls were a boring cream color that the overhead florescent lights reflected off.

Tucker flattened himself up against the wall and looked up the stairwell, then pressed his finger to his lips. He held up three fingers, then pointed upward. I nodded in understanding that three men were standing guard. I gathered a ball of magic in my hand, ready for anything. Behind me, Grayson pulled his throwing stars from his inner pocket. Ashryn's bow was at the ready, notched with an arrow, and Nova pulled her gloves off and shoved them into her pocket. Purple sparks gathered on her fingertips.

I expected Tuck to summon his swords, but he didn't. Instead, he ran up the first flight of stairs soundlessly. He came up behind the first guard, wrapped his hands around the man's chest, and threw him over the railing. The man plummeted down the center of the stairs, and from behind me, an arrow shot straight into his chest. Before he hit the ground, he burst into black ash. *Thralls!* I should've known by the outfit. During my last encounter with Alataris' Thralls, they'd all been wearing black track pants, neon yellow shirts, and dark sunglasses.

These weren't men at all. They used to be witches but were now soulless, mindless soldiers Alataris made using his black magic. Another body came flying back toward us, and I didn't hesitate. I threw a ball of magic, hitting him right in the face. We didn't wait to see if he turned to ash. We just kept on following Tuck higher and higher. When we were only one flight of stairs from the top, one of Alataris' Thralls smacked a big red button on the side of the wall. The lights went out, and an alarm wailed to life. Overhead, the exit lighting flashed on and off like a red strobe light. The door we'd come in flew open and banged into the cement wall. Thralls flooded into the stairwell. My heart leapt into my throat, and I ran up the stairs after Tuck.

"Move, move, move!" he called out to me and the rest of the crew. Just as I was about to reach him, he leapt up over my head. His wings shot out of his back, and he dove down behind Ashryn, who was bringing up the back.

I turned. "Tucker!"

Grayson pushed both of his hands into my shoulders. "Keep going. The faster we all get out, the faster he gets out."

I leaned over the railing just a second longer, fighting against Gray's hold. Tuck was like an avenging angel with his wings of fire and his flaming swords. He landed behind Ashryn on the stairs and held his swords at the ready. The Thralls attacked in a wave. Tuck swung his blades like they were extensions of his arms. Black dust rained down whichever way he moved. Yet the Thralls kept pushing him farther up the stairs.

"Zinnia, get to the door!" This time, Grayson shoved me harder, and I had to take my eyes off Tuck. On the landing, only a few steps away, stood two more guards. I closed my eyes for a second, remembering the blades Tuck had made for me. White beams of light glowed in my hands, then suddenly, the hilts hit my palms. I wrapped my fingers around them and threw the one in my right hand followed by the one in my left. I didn't know how I summoned them. All I knew was Tucker needed me. My adrenaline pumped through my body and my magic answered the call.

They spun like Frisbees at the Thralls. The first one smacked right into its chest, exploding it into black dust, and the second slashed across the Thrall's neck. It clucked its throat a second before it too turned to ash. The two blades didn't stop spinning. They turned around and headed back toward me like a boomerang. One flew right by my head. I reached out and snagged it. The blade stopped less than an inch away from Gray's face.

"Nice catch there."

I pulled it back and opened my other hand for the second blade. The moment it hit my palm I turned to run. "Let's move."

The muscles in my legs burned, and I sucked in panting breaths. *I have got to start doing more cardio.* When I reached the door, I pressed the handle down, but it didn't budge. I rammed my shoulder into it over and over again. Each time I boomed against the door, pain shot through one side of my body to the other. "It won't move."

"Step back." Grayson raced past me with his vampire speed and nailed the door head-on.

It blasted wide-open, and I ran out onto the roof of the Space Needle. Freezing rain poured down on me. My hair clung to the sides of my face as I spun around, ready for what was to come next. Nova charged through the door, followed by Ashryn.

I waited for him to come through next. "Where's Tuck?"

No sooner had the question left my mouth did Tuck fly through the door and slam it shut. He pressed his back to it as loud pounding came from the other side. The door opened just a fraction, and he braced his legs and shoved backward. "Gray, hold the door."

Grayson ran to his side, then pushed his hands to it and spread his legs. "Got it."

"This might hurt." Tucker held his hands out, and fire flew from his palms like blowtorches. He aimed them around the edge of the door, melting the metal frame and the steal door together inch by inch.

"Getting hot, mate." Sweat rolled down the sides of Gray's face and dripped from his chin.

"Just another second." Tucker pressed his lips together and focused on the bottom corner of the door. "And . . . we're . . . done."

Grayson leapt back and shook out his fingers, then blew across his palms. "Let's not do that again."

Boom. Boom. Boom. The Thralls rammed at the door as we all stood there breathless and soaking wet.

Grayson pushed his dark locks back from his face. He glanced at the door. "How do we get the key and get out of here?"

Nova yelled over the pounding rain. "Hades said there was a combination lock on the roof. Let's spread out and look for it."

This wasn't going to be like walking across the street. The roof had a slight slope to it, which gave it that dome-like look. I held my hands out and stepped carefully, trying not to slip off one of the tallest buildings I'd ever seen in person. "Okay."

I began walking toward the edge. The metal under my feet looked like a racetrack. Each lane was a different color and connected. In my mind, I pictured the top of the Space Needle looking like a CD with each track connecting around it in a perfect circle. On the inside track, there were different symbols carved into bronze-like metal. They seemed so familiar, but I couldn't place them. After that came Roman numerals in silver, then lastly in the golden track were all the phases of the moon.

"Guys!" I rubbed the water from my eyes. "I found it."

Grayson and Tuck were the first to get close to me. Tucker looked around. "Found what?"

"The combination lock. It's . . . well, it's the roof."

"What?" He glanced down at his feet. Nova and Ashryn strolled up next to Gray.

I pointed to each of the tracks. "Look, I'm not sure what the first signs mean. They look familiar, but the second one is definitely Roman numerals, and the third looks like phases of the moon."

Nova bent down and ran her fingers over the sign at her feet. It resembled a sideways sixty-nine. "Cancer." She moved to the next one that started with a small circle with a cursive lowercase *n* attached to it. "Leo." She straightened her stance. "It's zodiac signs."

I held my hands out to my sides, looking at each of them. "Oh my God, it's a date. A specific date. With the phase of the moon on that date."

Tucker threw his hands up into the air. "How the hell are we going to know a date that's important to Alataris? It could be anything. The first day he killed someone, the day he got into power, the day he killed his father and took the throne. Who knows?"

"Wait a second. Maybe we don't have to guess." I squatted down and pressed my hand to the cold soaking metal. "Maybe all we need is a spell."

Boom! Again, the Thralls crashed at the door. The

center of it dented in. Tucker looked from the door back at me. "Whatever you're going to do, you need to do it fast."

There was no way of knowing what Alataris was thinking, but if I could get a glimpse into his mind for even a moment to see what he was thinking. "If I use a spell, I might be able to get the combination."

"Don't you think other witches would've tried a spell to crack the combination?" Nova looked from me toward the door. Water ran down the hair, sticking to the sides of her face.

"Yes, but what if they were only going after the combo, not insight into him?" I stepped out into the middle of the roof and held my hands out at my sides.

"I hate to interrupt you, ladies, but do something now." Grayson hurried back toward the door and forced his back to it. Ashryn joined him. They both bounced every time the door was slammed against.

I closed my eyes and called my magic to my hands. I felt it swirling around my body, an array of powers I'd gotten from the other queens but hadn't worn off yet. "Moon and stars bring me your magic from afar. Lend me your power, and grant me sight of times past under your light. Bless me with visions of the one I seek, give me the knowledge of that which I seek."

When I opened my eyes, the rain had stopped, and

the others were nowhere to be found. *What did I do?* Had I sent myself to another point in time? There standing in front of me was Alataris. I sucked in a breath and took a step back. I glanced around, looking for a place to hide, then I froze. Alataris looked so different than the last time I'd seen him. Only days ago he'd looked gaunt and skinny with ill-fitting clothing and long spider-like limbs. Now the man standing before me wasn't like that. He might even be considered *handsome.* He had thick dark hair combed back from his face and well-made black trousers falling from his slim hips down to polished dress shoes. One side of his dress shirt hung out from his waistband, while the other was tucked in. He tilted his head back and looked up at the stars. A bouquet of wildflowers hung limply in his hands, and a single tear rolled down his cheek.

He looked devastated as he dropped to his knees and opened his mouth in an agonizing bellow. "Why, why, why, Catherine?"

I took a step toward him and waved my hand. He didn't look up. I moved in closer and kneeled across from him, convinced I was in a vision of the past. Suddenly, he sprung to his feet and marched forward. I held my hand out, trying to stop him, but he passed right through me the way a ghost would pass through a wall.

"Damn you, Catherine." He slammed his fist down to the ground, and the many pieces of the roof started spinning. The bronze circle with the zodiac signs spun to the right, the silver ring with the Roman numerals spun to the left, and the last ring with the moons on it spun to the right. Alataris bowed his head and took a necklace off his neck and held it up. An old skeleton key hung from a long thin golden chain. He stood with his arms out to his sides. "Remember this day, remember this time."

I rushed forward, trying to see how the combination lined up. The bronze stopped on the sign for Libra, which was two parallel lines running together. The top line had a small hump in it. Next, the Roman numeral stopped on . . .

"Zinnia!"

I turned toward the voice. "Tuck?"

His voice sounded like he was yelling through water. "Wake up, we need you."

Need me? No, they couldn't. I had to get two more numbers. I glanced over toward Alataris as the numbers ticked by one by one. Twenty-five, twenty-six, twenty-seven . . . I sucked in a breath. Twenty-eight?

Before I could see it stop, my whole body was jerked sideways, and my head rolled around on my shoulders. Drops of water smacked into my face, and I peeked open my eyes, even though I didn't remember closing them. Tucker had his hands on my shoulders. The heat from his body pressed into me, and I shook my head. "What happened?"

"I don't know. Your eyes went full black, and you just stopped moving." His eyes were round with concern, and he looked me over. "Are you okay? Did you get the combo?"

Combo? Boom! I snapped to attention. The haze I was in was all but forgotten. "Right, the combo." I shrugged out of his grip and moved to stand at the very edge of the roof where I remembered Alataris standing. At my feet was a small arrow that was only about an inch big. We never would've found it at night in the middle of a storm had I not seen it for myself. The wind whipped around me, and I stood with my legs apart, trying to keep my balance. My hair flew across my face.

I raised my fist over my head and slammed it down on top of the arrow. The rings groaned as they slowly started to spin. I pointed to the bronze ring, which was farthest away from me. "Nova, stop it at Libra."

"Stop it?" Her eyes widened, but she ran forward. "How?"

In my vision, Alataris used a spell, but I didn't think it would work for us. "Blast it."

She held her hands out in front of her, and purple

sparks shot from her fingers. She shoved it down into the first ring. The top one grinded to a halt at the Libra sign. Next was the Roman numeral. I didn't know what he stopped the number on, only that it was close to the twenty-eighth. "Okay, Gray, stop it on twenty-eight."

"I'm no magical unicorn. How do you expect me to stop it?"

I knew he was right. "Fine, I'll do it." I reached out my hand toward the silver spinning ring and shoved my magic into it. When I tried to stop it on the twenty-eight, it spun even faster. *Damn it! Wrong guess.*

"I can't hold this much longer, Zin." Nova's whole body quaked from head to toe.

"Okay!" *Get it together, Zin.* I focused all my attention on the silver ring and stopped it on the twenty-ninth. With my magic holding it, it grinded to a halt. As long as I kept my magic flowing through it, I knew it wouldn't move.

"One more, Zin," Tucker called out. When he met my wide eyes, he must've seen I had no idea. He pressed his lips together. "What's the year?"

"What?"

"You've got September twenty-ninth. For what year?" He called to me as he straddled the golden ring.

The center of the door burst open, and hands shot through it. Grayson and Ashryn hunched over, holding the door in place. Gray cursed. "Now! This needs to happen now!"

"Two thousand and two." Exactly sixteen years ago . . .

Tuck pulled his phone from his pocket and started typing. I couldn't believe it. "We don't have time for texting Niche."

He summoned his sword from the palm of his hands, then spun it around and stabbed it through the metal, stopping the ring from moving on the last quarter moon. The gears in the roof began to click and move. "How did you know it was the quarter moon?"

He held his phone up. "Google."

I rolled my eyes. "Seriously?"

"What else were we going to do?"

Before I could answer, the needlepoint slowly began to lower back into the building. The tip was nearly completely down when it stopped, and the side of the Needle peeled back like a flower opening to the sun. The key floated in a light pink beam of light.

I looked around at our group. "Who's going to grab it?"

"I don't care who grabs it." Grayson pulled one of his throwing stars from his pocket and slashed out at the snatching hands. "Do it now. This door is going to go."

"Go, Tuck!" I pointed toward the key.

Tucker turned on his heels and ran headlong at the key. The gears below the roof began to quake and clink together.

"Hurry up."

He dove forward with his hand extended out. The second he wrapped his fingers around the chain, the needlepoint snapped shut, closing a millimeter away from the bottom of the key. He skidded to a halt on the other side of the roof just as the door to the roof was forced wide-open, sending Ashryn and Grayson stumbling back. Thralls flooded out toward us. I summoned my magic to the palms of my hands.

The gears below the roof clicked once more, and a tick started. The silver, gold, and bronze rings vibrated below my feet. I locked gazes with Tucker a second before the rings all spiraled in opposite directions like a top. Ashryn, Grayson, and Nova flew off the roof like rag dolls. I couldn't hold myself any longer. My body was jerked to the side, and my feet went flying up over my head. I reached out and tried to grab onto anything to stop me from soaring off the roof.

The last thing I saw was Tucker reaching out for me. "Zinnia!"

CHAPTER 29

I extended my hands out to try and meet Tucker's outstretched fingers. He leapt over the side of the building and dove for me. The ground rushed up toward me. I didn't know if he was going to make it. I called upon my magic once more, praying it'd work. Thralls all spilled over the edge of the roof, falling like dominoes toward us. I couldn't see the others and didn't know what happened to them. I sent silvery swirls of magic shooting all around, latching on to everyone. I pictured the next point on the map in my head. "By the grace of lady moon, this trip I take very soon. Return us now to that which we seek, the sacred piece of the dragon to keep."

A bright light opened in the ground and I closed my eyes, bracing for the painful impact I knew would come.

Instead, I felt myself falling through it. My heart-stopping drop turned to a slow drift. I was in a sea of blue light, floating the way I did in the ocean. The others drifted into view, all of them looking as shocked as I was. Time slowed. For a moment, there were no Thralls and we all weren't falling to our deaths. Sure, Tuck might've been able to save me, but what about the others? My arms and legs pinwheeled in slow motion, and my hair wafted around my face. The frantic pounding of my heart relaxed and felt like I was swimming in a warm bath.

Then everything sped back up as I crashed through the other side of the blue area. I landed flat on my back on soft, deep sand. The smell of food, horses, and manure made me wrinkle my nose. When I gazed up at the sky, I realized I wasn't looking at the sky at all. Above was a dome with industrial steel beams running across it.

"Ladies and gentlemen, I give you our princess," the announcer boomed over the loudspeaker.

The crowd erupted into fits of cheers. *What the heck is going on?* I rolled to my side and groaned. I ached all over, and I could feel the threads of exhaustion making my eyelids heavy. *Did I use too much magic?*

A blinding spotlight shined down on me, and I held my hand up, trying to block it out. A horse trampled so close I nearly fell over. The crowd cheered and laughed. My feet felt sluggish as I dragged them through the thick sand. When I looked into the crowd, I noticed each area was split up by color. A flag with an emblem on it hung over each section. People sat all around with paper crowns on to match their part as well as small flags. And then it hit me . . . *medieval times . . . nooooo.*

I spun in a circle, looking out at everyone cheering and waving. *Where is Tucker and the rest of them? Did the spell I used go so wrong that we're all separated now?* When I looked down at myself, I groaned for a whole new reason. Pink satin and lace draped loosely from my body all the way down to the floor. *Pink? Really?* What the hell kind of trick was this? Another horse came so close to me I stumbled back. Before I hit the ground, two strong hands caught me and righted me.

"Careful."

I spun on my heels and smiled. "Tucker, thank God."

"I wouldn't thank anyone yet." He stood before me dressed in an old knight costume.

I arched my eyebrow at him. "A knight? How *appropriate.*"

"Have you looked at yourself . . . queen?" He plucked at something on my head. "Nice tiara."

I reached up to the top of my head. There was indeed a tiara. "What happened?"

"Best I figure is whatever spell you cast sent us to where the vault is, but at the same time we ended up in"—he swallowed and sighed—"in costume."

"Where are the others?" I turned to look for them. To my right, two pretend knights were engaged in a fake battle. To my left, two others were waving to the crowd and smiling, all the while tossing carnations into the audience.

"I don't know, but we have to go." He grabbed my hand and began dragging me toward the tunnel when everything went completely silent. I froze with my heart thundering in my chest.

My hand shook in Tucker's grasp. "Why are they all looking at us?"

"I don't know. Keep moving." He tugged me once more. The crowd rose to their feet as one. Like soldiers, they marched out of the rows and up the aisles without speaking a word. Their feet pounded—*boom, boom, boom*—like a rhythmic drum. Even the fake knights mounted their horses and made their way out of the arena.

A slow clapping came from the other side of the room, followed by a lifeless giggle. A chill went down my spine. I knew that laugh. Sometimes I heard it in my nightmares. I looked toward where the clapping came from . . . Ophelia.

Alataris' daughter was the stuff nightmares were

made of. She was cold, calculating, and unfeeling. Two long black braids hung down on either side of her pale face. Her eyes were black as night, and when she looked at me, I felt as though winter was upon me. She walked down two steps. "Did you think you'd get the key and this would be a piece of cake?"

I threw my arms up and shrugged. "Yeah, well, kind of."

Ophelia canted her head to the side. "Interesting." She lifted her hand and snapped her fingers. Thralls ran down each of the aisles. We were completely surrounded, and I didn't know where we were going to go or what we were going to do.

Tuck summoned his swords to his hands. His flames danced all the way down from his shoulder to the tips of the blades. "Stay close."

I pressed my back to his and held my hands out, envisioning the dual blades he'd made just for me. With two little white flashes of light, they appeared in my palms. I wrapped my fingers around them and held them up.

Behind me, Tuck froze. "How'd you do that?"

I shrugged. "You do it."

"It's old phoenix shifter magic. It's not common."

Why was he bringing this up now? "Um, do you think we can focus here for a second?"

"Oh, right." Tucker threw his sword out at the first line of Thralls as they approach. One after another, they disappeared into dust. The sword spun and embedded itself into the stone stairs. Tuck held his hand out, and the sword disappeared into thin air then reappeared in his hand.

"Move with me, move in time, dance alone to the desires in my mind," Ophelia yelled from high above us. All at once the Thralls flooded onto the arena floor. I threw my blade out and watched it spiral through the crowd of Thralls. Each one bellowed and crumbled into nothingness. Tucker too was doing the same thing, yet they seemed to be closing in on us.

I was out of breath and exhausted. The muscles in my arms burned with exertion. Each time I threw my blades and caught them it hurt a little more. "This isn't working."

"I know." He took off running circles around me in a blur of fire. Flames circled around us, holding the Thralls back just enough for us to move. And then it hit me.

"I have an idea." I dropped my blades down and called my powers to my hands.

"Tell me."

"Can you make the ring of fire go higher? Like, make it a wall?" I spun around to face him.

He didn't say anything, didn't move. He was beautiful and deadly with his flaming swords, wild hair, and molten honey eyes. Large rips marred his shirt, and I could see his tan skin underneath. The flames shot straight up twenty feet around us.

We each took a step toward each other, and then another and another. We stood so close not even a blade would come between us. "You ready?"

"Always." He nodded.

I threw my hands up, sending my magic out. The sand rose off the floor. I could feel every grain of it, and one by one, I forced them to clump together just enough, then shoved them through the wall of fire. The fire alarms went off, and the sprinkler system that ran across the ceiling kicked to life. *Perfect.*

With the rest of my magic, I forced the falling water to cyclone just outside the fire. Three layers of elements protected us from Ophelia and her Thralls. But it wasn't enough to only be protected. We had to make it out of here with the dragon heart scale. I threw the sand right through the fire, where it melted together into molten glass. Then I shot it through the water. Shards of razor-sharp glass exploded out like shrapnel. It flew in all directions, taking down Thrall after Thrall until the arena was emptied of them all. I dropped the water down, then Tucker let his fire wall fall.

I turned, ready to face off against Ophelia, but she'd disappeared. The only people left were Tucker and me. I sucked in deep panting breaths. Tucker hunched over and did the same. "Wow."

I nodded. "Thanks."

"That was . . . just damn." He shook his head, then wrapped his arms around me and pulled me close to his chest.

"We just have to find the vault now." I pressed my face into him and closed my eyes.

"Um, Zinnia?"

"Yeah?"

He ran his fingers through my hair. "You're standing on it."

CHAPTER 30

I dropped my hold on him and took a step back while looking down at my feet. "The vault is the whole floor? You've got to be kidding me."

At the center of the arena, the floor met in a deep seam. Two half-moons lined up against the seam, creating a circle with a key hole in the middle of it. I extended my hand out to him and wiggled my fingers. "Key, please?

He whipped the key from his neck and dropped it in my palm. "Do the honors."

I squatted down on one knee and shoved the key into the lock and turned it to the right. The clanking gears ground together, and the floor opened at the seam and slid back underneath the seating. I peeked over the edge into a room that glowed yellow from the mounds of gold and treasures. It was the size of a football field.

My jaw dropped, and I couldn't stop staring. "How are we going to find it in all this before more Thralls get here? What if Ophelia comes back? What if—"

He held up a finger, and his lips pulled up in that half smirk he gave me every time he was thinking something naughty. He pulled his phone from his pocket, hit the screen a couple of times, then held it to his ear. "Beckett, we need transport." He glanced around at the treasure. "How big? Let's just say massive. Yeah, I'll ping you my location and you get us back to the school. Okay?" He nodded, then ended the call.

"You can't take all of this back to the school. It's not possible."

His chest rumbled with a chuckle. "Watch me."

CHAPTER 31

TUCKER

"**E**xplain to me why you decided to smash my fountain again?" Matteaus crossed his arms while he stood on top of a pile of gold that'd fallen into the middle of Evermore Academy. The fountain was somewhere under that pile . . . smashed to pieces.

"It wasn't that I meant to smash it. It just kind of happened." I held my hands up in a *what could I do* motion. Though the city was under more than six feet of snow, the courtyard only had a thin coating. Well, before we dropped Alataris' entire treasure into it. I toed a ruby the size of my fist. It rolled down a small mound, sending golden coins skittering in all directions and making them clank together.

He pinched the bridge of his nose and sighed. "My school is not a bank!"

"And I didn't mean to make it one." I bent over and scooped an emerald off the ground. "We couldn't stay very long. Ophelia was there, and who knew when Alataris would show up? And how were we going to sift through all this stuff to find the dragon heart scale? And once we did find it, what were we going—"

Matteaus held his hand up, cutting off my words. "Enough. Just . . . just clean up the mess, kid."

"But I thought you might want to use it." I hedged, hoping he would tell me exactly how to get rid of it all. Even back in my home kingdom of Cindelore I wasn't allowed to be in the treasury. This was years of saving, stealing, and working toward an unmasked fortune. Who knew what untold secrets lay within the mound of gold coins Alataris had collected?

"This is chump change." Matteaus turned and began striding away. The tips of his huge black wings dragged on the ground behind him. Black feathers fluttered to the ground, sticking out against the white snow and golden coins. "Clean up . . . now."

I spun in a slow circle, looking over the courtyard. Was there ever going to be a time when we weren't crashing into the fountain? I didn't think so. Footsteps sounded behind me, crunching through the gold. The warmth that spread through my chest told me it was her

. . . Zinnia. The girl who both tortured me and gave me peace.

"Hey." Her voice was sultry and sweet all at the same time. When I spun to look at her, she shoved her hands into her jacket pockets. She titled her head in the direction Matteaus had gone in. "Was he pissed?"

I shrugged. "No more than usual." I knew Matteaus was getting tired of the mess we were making of Evermore Academy, but at the same time, it couldn't be helped. We had to find the scale, and we didn't have time to do it before. I'd like to think that one day this would all be over, and we would be free of Alataris.

"I'm glad the others made it back okay. Gray looked pissed when we got here." She fidgeted with the hem of her shirt.

"Thanks to your quick thinking. Sending them here was incredible."

She wrapped her arms around her midsection. "I honestly didn't mean to. It just kind of happened."

"Zin, don't take this the wrong way, but you've got to have more faith in yourself. You're gaining more control over your powers every day." In truth, she was incredible to watch. Every day, she mastered new powers, new spells, and grew more confident. *I just wish she saw it.*

"It would've been better if I could've figured out a way

to find the scale before." She pulled a book out from under her arm and held it out to me. "Professor Davis just gave this to me. It might help you look through all this stuff."

I held it up and read the title. "*Spelling out Spells?*"

Red tinged her cheeks, and she bit her bottom lip. "Yeah, I lost the first copy in the bus fire. I had to go and tell her. Somehow, she summoned another from thin air and gave it to me. I got through more than half of it."

"Is that how you were able to do those spells all on your own?"

She nodded. "Yeah, I just got lucky, I guess."

I handed the book back to her and smiled. "Or you're just that good."

"I don't know about that. I fly by the seat of my pants a lot." She gave a light chuckle. "I'm still surprised the elemental powers Tabi gave me are holding up."

"I have a theory about that." I plucked up a gold coin and tossed it in the air, then caught it. "What if you're a different kind of Siphon Witch?"

"What do you mean?" She arched her eyebrow and looked at me like I was crazy. This was the first time the tension between us wasn't burning out of control. Instead, it was a comfortable undercurrent of connection between us, an ebb and flow I relished. I wished we'd share it more often.

"Meaning, what if you siphon power but when you use it you keep some of it for your own?"

Her jaw dropped just a little. "That's not possible."

"You should know by now that anything in Evermore is possible. But that would make you the most—"

"Powerful witch of them all." She turned away from me, and I could feel the tension return to her body. Small tremors ran over her from head to toe. "No, this can't happen."

I knew exactly what she was feeling. The shock, the fear, it wasn't going to be easy on her. I walked up behind her and placed my hands on her shoulders. "It'll be okay."

She spun around and looked up at me with wide eyes. "How—" A group of students walked out into the courtyard and laughed as they kicked at the coins and threw jewels back and forth like a baseball. Zinnia took a small step away from me, then lowered her voice. "How is this going to be okay?"

"Because I'm here to help you, and with the two of us working together, we'll be unstoppable. I just know it."

"Hey, look. I'm metal man." A scrawny boy with black brillo-like hair and glasses too big for his face held his arms out, and the coins flew toward him like he was a magnet. They clung to him one by one until he was the incredible hulk of gold coins. His friends all hunched over laughing.

Zinnia looked at them with longing in her face, as though she wished she could be anywhere but here. Stuck in a life she hadn't asked for and wasn't prepared to handle, what a pair we made. A few weeks ago I'd felt that exact same way.

A smile played on her lips as she gazed at the other students. "They're so carefree."

"I'm sure they have their own worries just like everyone else."

She shrugged. "I suppose so."

"Look, Zin, after we fix this whole mess with the dragon and the scale—"

"Speaking of that, we have to find the dragon scale in all this mess. I kind of had an idea for that." She held her hands out to her sides and gathered her magic in her palms.

"Zinnia, wait." I grabbed her wrist, stopping her from going any further.

"Everything okay?" She glanced down at my hands wrapped around hers.

"Before we do this, I-I just want to tell you something." I looked down at my wrist, wanting to rip the thick bracelet from my skin and show her exactly what she meant to me. This secret pressed on me like a weight sitting on my chest. I dropped her hands and wrapped my fingers around the snap that held the leather cuff together.

"Tuck? What's going on?" Her brow furrowed in confusion. I was ready to tell her everything. I wanted to tell her everything.

The words were on the tip of on tongue. *Zinnia, it's me, I'm your soul mate.* I peered around the courtyard, making sure we were alone. Hidden in the shadows, or at least he thought he was hidden, stood Beckett with his arms crossed over his chest. His surfer blond hair hung from his head in a messy tangle of waves. Small icicles hung from the tips of his hair, and his coat was covered in a thick layer of snow. Dark bags hung under his eyes, and his cheeks looked hollow from hunger. He took a small step from the shadows and motioned for me to join him.

Would my life always be like this? Torn between the role I was born into and the girl I wanted? I dropped my hand from my bracelet and sighed. "I just want to make sure we're good, that's all."

"Oh, um, yeah. We're good." She cast her eyes down at the ground and kicked at the handle of a gold-plated shield.

I tucked my finger under her chin and raised her face

to meet my gaze. "I wouldn't want anything to, you know, come between us."

"Oh, don't worry." She shrugged. "There isn't anything between us to worry about. Is there?"

I shook my head. "Zinnia," I whispered. "There will always be something between us . . . always."

Her lip tilted up at the corner. "Yeah, maybe."

"Tuck, I need to talk to you," Beckett called to me.

I didn't want to move from her. "I'll be right back." When I turned to run toward Beck, the coins jingled beneath my feet.

"Hey, Tuck!"

I spun on my heels to face her. "Yeah?"

She spread her arms out wide. "What is lost I now wish to find. Open my eyes through the golden divine. Direct me to what I seek. Use my vision and give me a peek."

Gold sparks shot from her eyes while tendrils of her magic spilled from her palms and ran over the treasure like snakes in all directions. The students who'd been playing only moments ago scurried from the courtyard back under an archway.

A smile played on her lips. "Ah, there you are."

All the way in the back corner of the courtyard, the silvery lines of her magic spun together in a cone shape, forming a drill. It shot down into the ground, sending gold coins, jewels, and precious stones flying in all different directions. They smacked into the walls surrounding the courtyard, hitting students as they passed by and denting the brick walls. A hole opened up within the gold hill. The tornado of magic dipped down and scooped up a white object the size of a plate from the bottom of the pile and flew it back toward her outstretched palm.

Her magic receded back into her body as she wrapped her fingers around the object. "I believe we now have the scale."

Is there anything you can't do?

She sauntered over to me and held the scale out. "Mission accomplished." It was a shining pearly white with light blue all around the rim of it.

I gently took it from her. "I think I expected it to be bigger."

"Yeah, me too." She beamed. "But at least now we have the scale."

I held the scale tightly in my grasp. "Thanks for finding this. It could've taken us hours."

"Tuck, man. I gotta go," Beckett snapped at me.

I didn't turn to answer him. Instead, I looked right at Zinnia. "I'll meet you in the library in a sec."

"Okay." She peeked up at me from under those thick eyelashes, then winked and strutted away. I followed her with my gaze, watching her mesmerizing hips sway in those tight black leggings of hers. I was convinced they were made to torture me or hypnotize me. Either way, I couldn't move.

The moment she disappeared into the hallway leading to the library, I turned and jogged over to where Becket leaned against the stone pillar. He ran his thumb across his bottom lip. "You've got a bit of drool just there."

"Oh, right here?" I made a show of running my finger over my mouth, then shoved him playfully. "Shut up."

Beckett shook his head and chuckled. "You got it bad."

"Am I that obvious?" I glanced around, making sure no one could hear us.

"Nah, I just pay attention."

"Well, let's just keep it under wraps for now." I sucked in a deep breath, then blew it out. "What's going on?"

"It's Tabi. I don't know how much longer she can help control the seas. Her power is draining. The tides are shaky at best. She's going to collapse soon, and when she does . . ."

"Major destruction?" I stabbed my hands through my hair. "How long do we have?"

Beckett shrugged. "Five hours, maybe less."

I froze, and my heart leapt up into my throat. "Five hours?"

When he looked at me, his eyes were deadly serious, and his lips were pressed into a thin line. "Yeah."

"Well, what did Poseidon say?" I shuffled from one foot to the other.

"Say? We can't get to him. He's been battling with that giant since you left. Tuck, we have to get that ice dragon back. We are out of time. I know he's powerful and all, but how long can one supernatural battle against a half Titan and win? I don't want to risk it. Do you?" He gathered a blue ball in the center of his palm and opened up a portal just to his right. "Go do what you gotta do. We're counting on you. No pressure or anything."

"Yeah, no pressure." I rolled my eyes.

Beckett clapped me on the shoulder. "Good luck." He stepped through the portal and disappeared. But before I could move away, he popped his head back through. "Oh yeah, and don't die."

I held the dragon scale even tighter. "Thanks."

CHAPTER 32

ZINNIA

Niche paced back and forth in front of me. She went from nervously wringing her hands while she paced to flat out marching each time she changed direction. Normally her glasses were sliding down her nose, barely holding on, but now they were downright crooked. Her fire engine red hair had tumbled out of its tight bun and was currently in a messy ponytail that fell all the way down to her waist. We sat in a small glassed-in room at the back of the library. There was a TV mounted on the wall in the corner. The human media was having a field day with images of rough seas. Pictures of coast after coast flashed.

The news anchor spoke in a deep, grave voice. "In other news, diplomats from all over the world are meeting in an unprecedented emergency summit in . . ."

He paused. "Nebraska? I guess the farther inland, the safer . . . To discuss the weather patterns the entire world is now feeling."

I tuned him out and focused on the massive waves bearing down on the beaches around the world. The countdown had begun. We needed to find the dragon, or Alataris would destroy us all.

Niche slammed her hand down on the map we'd gotten from the Furies. "I don't understand how his location could just disappear. You said it yourself you saw the moving dot."

"I know, but the way I figure it, Alataris has connected it to someone and wiped himself off it. That's the only explanation that makes sense." I walked over to stand next to her and peer down at the new map. It used to have all the locations of his vault and the key and his hidden floating island. Now all it held was a very old map of the United States.

Tucker shoved through the door in that exact moment, then slammed it shut behind him. "Bad news. We have exactly five hours until Tabi burns out."

I motioned to the images of the turbulent oceans. "I think we've got a lot less than that."

"Wait a second." Niche's hand splayed over the map. "If this thing is still connected to Alataris, then we might have a chance to find his location."

"What do you mean? I thought if he hid it on the map there's no finding him now." I didn't want to let myself hope there was a way to fix this. We'd been working toward this moment. I didn't want it to slip away.

"Yes, he hid it on the map, but his magic is all over it. Like a footprint. If we could tap into that somehow, I might be able to find him." She shoved her hand into the pocket of her jeans and pulled a long silver chain from it. At the bottom of the chain hung an amethyst stone. The light purple crystal twirled around slowly and I could see every vein, color, and reflection of light.

I thought I might've seen her with one in Hexia, but I couldn't be sure. "What's that?"

Niche pinched the end of the chain between her thumb and forefinger and let the crystal dangle over the map. "It's a pendulum."

I reached out, ready to touch the crystal, when Niche swatted my hand away.

"Don't touch it. I have to concentrate." She closed her eyes and bowed her head.

I sat and waited for it to do something—to move, or sway, or fly out of her grip and embed itself into the map somewhere. I whispered, "Is it supposed to do something?"

Tucker nodded. "It's supposed to drop where he is."

But the stone didn't move, not even a tick. I stared at

it, willing it to show us where he was, where the dragon was, but most of all where my mom was. I knew wherever he was, he would have her with him.

Niche growled and slammed it down on the table. "This isn't working. We need some kind of catalyst."

"What do you mean?" Tucker narrowed his eyes at the pendulum.

"If we could dip the crystal in his blood, or even Ophelia's, that mixed with his magic on the map might work. But we need both his magic imprint on this map and his blood."

I threw my hands up. "Well, unless he suddenly became a good Samaritan and donated a bunch of blood to the local supernatural blood bank, I'd say we are out of luck."

Tucker stood with one arm crossed over his chest and the other arm leaning on it while he ran his hand over his bottom lip. "Maybe not."

Niche's head snapped up. "What do you mean?"

"Well, what if we had someone who shares the same powers as him? Would that be enough of a connection to find him?" When he met my gaze, I could've sworn I saw a flash of regret.

"Are you saying I have to douse that crystal in my blood?" I looked from her to Tuck and back again.

Niche nodded. "It might just work. We don't have much other choice."

I held my hand out, then rolled up my sleeve. "Do what you need to do."

Tuck leaned over the table and held his hands out. "Wait a second. Once we find his location, we have to leave right away before the island moves again, right?"

Niche nodded. "Right."

"So we need to get the crew together, and we need a way to actually get there." Tucker's eyes bore into mine. "Do you think you could get us there?"

I shook my head. "Getting to the vault was lucky. If I try to take us there now, we could end up in the ocean. And I'm going to be direct here. I almost drowned once this week. I'd rather not do it again."

His lips pressed into a thin line, and the muscle in his jaw ticked. The loose strands of his dark auburn hair fell over his forehead while his honey eyes turned from liquid gold to red and back again. "I wouldn't want to ever see you go through that again. So, what's the plan?" He turned toward Niche.

She leaned back on her heels. "Look, guys. I've got to level with you. Grayson, Ash, and Nova are all out helping Brax and Adrienne deal with the state of emergency. There's a lot of people out there hurting. And, well, Beckett and Tabi are still in Alaska. That only leaves you two. To face Alataris alone." She shook her head. "And I can't let only two of you go."

Tucker shook his head. "You've got no other choice. We can sneak in, save the dragon, and leave before anyone realizes what's happened. But if we don't go now, then all this . . ." He waved his hand over the map. "None of it will matter if we don't stop it now."

She sucked in a deep breath and hesitantly nodded. "Very well." She lifted her hand and waved it in a circle. A white fog drifted from the floor, filling the room with smoke.

Professor Davis stood before me, waving away the fog and coughing. "Honestly, Niche, how many times do I have to tell you to stop doing . . ." She glance down at me. "Oh, Zinnia dear, so lovely to see you."

Her hair looked like a salt and pepper cotton ball all around her face, and her chubby cheeks were red with exertion.

I raised my eyebrows. "Hello, Professor. How are you?"

"Oh, I'm all right. I'd be even better if Niche wouldn't just summon me at will." When she put her hands on her hips, her long hunter green dress rustled. I couldn't understand how she'd be comfortable in a dress that had such a high stiff turtle neck and puffy sleeves that cinched in at her wrists.

"Come on, Elba. You know I wouldn't do it if it wasn't necessary." Niche rested both of her hands on the table and leaned over the map.

"Well, your little summoning power is all well and good until you interrupt someone while making their lunch." She crossed her arms over her chest.

"Please, Elba. You know I can only do it within the walls of the school and I wouldn't have done it if it wasn't an emergency. This is important. We only have a short time to get to Alataris; otherwise, the seas will rise up and a giant will be unleashed on the world. I don't think I need to tell you how dire our situation is."

Elba nodded and took her place next to Tucker. I stood waiting, watching what would come next. She lifted her hands and snapped her fingers at me. "Well, girl, what are you waiting for?"

I startled to action and walked around the table as quickly as I possibly could. "I'm here, I'm here."

Niche sighed and shook her head. "I don't like this. Not one bit. The others—"

"Are nowhere near here." I held my hand out to her. "Are you doing this or not?"

Tuck bent over, hiked up his pant leg, and pulled a knife from the side of his combat boot. "Here." He handed the jagged blade over to Niche.

I wagged my eyebrows at him and pointed toward

his boots. "Just walking around with that tucked in there? Must be comfortable."

He winked at me. "Like wearing a pair of slippers."

A sliding sting ran across the palm of my hand. "Ouch." I yanked it back from Niche's hand. A line of blood rose up from the gouge in my palm, and a wave of dizziness washed over me. "Did you really need to put a four-inch cut in my hand for just a bit of blood?"

Niche laid the crystal end of the pendulum across the wound. "Hold it for a minute."

I wrapped my fingers around the crystal, willing my magic to fuse with it. Drops of my blood dripped from my hand and coated the chain that dangled between my fingers. I closed my eyes, focusing all of my attention on the crystal. Tucker's warm, woodsy scent drifted over me . . . it wasn't distracting at all. Neither was the heat I could feel coming off of him or the fact I could tell how close he was to me. *Not distracting at all.*

"Zinnia! Are you listening to me?" Niche's sharp tone broke into my thoughts. With two fingers, she pinched the end of the chain and gave it a little tug. "You can let go now."

I shook myself. "Oh, right." I pried my fingers open one by one. The blood had already dried, making my hand stiff.

She pulled the pendulum from my grasp and held it

over the map. It started swinging in a circle. Little drops of my blood landed on the time-worn paper, yet the pendulum didn't stop moving. "Is it supposed to do something else, like land on the spot we are looking for?"

Tucker rocked back on his heels. "Yes, it is."

"Ugh, this should be working." Niche slammed her fists down on the table once more. Her whole body quaked, and she looked on the verge of losing it.

Professor Davis placed her hand on my shoulder. "Zinnia, do you remember the locator spell in the book I gave you?"

"Yes, but that's to find like small things around the house, not to find a floating island in the ocean." I motioned toward the map. "Unless . . ."

A wide smile spread across her face. "Unless what?"

My eyes darted around the map, looking at one blood drop to the next. "Unless I change it to something else?"

"Precisely." She nodded at me.

I held both my hands over the paper and forced pinpricks of my magic into each of my drops of blood. After all that I'd been through the past few days, I realized I may not always know what I was doing, but my instincts were strong and so was I. "Feel my magic woven by time, seek the one who matches mine. Track him now near or far. Through blood and magic reveal where you are."

The drops of blood on the map rose up off the paper and swirled together into one blob the size of a penny. It skittered across the page back and forth, then zigged and zagged, searching frantically. I held my breath. My heart raced in my chest and I tried to take deep breaths to calm down. This could be it, the moment we'd been working toward. The drop stopped on a single spot south of the equator, then it formed a perfect ring around a spot in the middle of the ocean just north of Australia. I sucked in a sharp breath. "Is that it?"

The four of us stood looking at each other with wide eyes. Professor Davis was the first to speak. "It is."

Shock, utter shock, overcame me. My jaw dropped open. "I-I guess we better go?"

Tucker nodded. "You ready for this?"

"Yes, I am." I was ready to face Alataris, I was ready to find my mom, and I was ready to free the dragon. The world was depending on us, and I was tired of waiting, tired of being afraid. My powers were growing, and it was time to embrace what they were becoming, what I was becoming.

Niche stepped in front of us. "You two listen to me right now. Get in, get the dragon, and get out."

"But my mom . . ." I looked from her at Tuck. "She's depending on me to come get her."

"Zinnia, your mother needs a world to come back to. We can't do two rescue missions at the same time. Get the dragon, get back here. When we're ready, we can *all* go to find her." Niche reached out and placed her hand on my shoulder. "Do you understand me?"

Though I nodded, I knew if I got even a hint of a chance at getting her, I was going to take it. "Okay," I lied.

Niche narrowed her eyes at me but didn't say anything. She took a small step back. "Very well, Professor Davis." She motioned to the wall. "If you would, please."

Professor Davis slapped her hands together and rubbed them back and forth. "Okay, here we go."

The palms of her hands glowed a neon purple as she bent over and placed her hand on the bottom of the glass wall beside us. She lifted her hand, drawing a purple line up and around, making an archway. In truth, it looked like a child's finger painting. When she connected the bottom of the door to the floor, the whole things glowed bright purple. Were all portals different based on the magic that made them? I had no idea, but it fascinated me.

Professor Davis walked behind Tucker and me. "Well, off you go."

Her hand pressed into the middle of my back, and she shoved me forward. My toe caught on the carpet, and I stumbled forward and grabbed onto Tuck.

He grabbed my arms and steadied me on my feet. "You ready?"

Was I? I nodded. "Absolutely."

His lips tilted up in that half cocky grin I loved. "Let's go."

I threw my shoulders back and held my head higher. I was ready to go into the portal to save the dragon, rescue my mom, and face Alataris . . . *piece of cake.*

CHAPTER 33

ZINNIA

The moment my combat boots hit the moss-covered ground, I knew we were in for an adventure. The floating island rocked back and forth like a toothpick in a bathtub . . . with a toddler.

Tucker stepped through the portal behind me and held his arms out. "Whoa."

"I wonder if he planned on the seas tossing his little hiding spot around." The thought of Alataris being stuck on this turbulent island trying to ride out the waves and suffering from sea sickness made me smile. I just wanted to see his tall, skinny ass clinging to the toilet seat, praying to the porcelain gods for relief.

All around us the palm trees swayed with the motion of the island. They rustled against each other, and their large leaves fell to the ground, piling up at the base of the thick tree trunks. If I hadn't known this island belonged to pure evil, I might've liked it. Lush bushes were spread for as far as the eye could see. Tropical flowers of the brightest colors adorned each one. Their fragrance drifted on the breeze. This far away from any civilization, the stars stood out like spotlights in a midnight sky. The air was thick and oppressively humid. Sweat trickled down my sides and back.

I peeled my jacket from my arms and tossed it to the ground. Tucker too peeled the sleeves of his jacket from his arms and tossed it down next to mine. His black V-neck T-shirt made his tan skin look even darker and gave his molten honey eyes a deadly look. He held his hands out to his sides, and the white light I'd grown so accustomed to appeared. The tips of his duel swords emerged from the palms of his hands, slowly rising until he wrapped his hands around the silver hilts. The phoenix that was etched into the base of the white blade matched the ones on the blades I'd learned to summon.

He looked around at the tropical forest, then nodded toward the castle. "You ready for this?"

"Yeah, I really think I am." I too summoned my blades to my hands. Each time I felt those hilts in my grasp, I grew more and more comfortable using them. The white metal matched Tucker's swords . . . a perfect match. The symbolism wasn't lost on me.

"Remember what Niche said about your mom?"

I froze, knowing I couldn't lie to him the way I lied to her. "Yeah?"

"Find her, Zin." His eyes softened, and his lips lifted into a half smile.

"But what about the dragon? What about saving all of us?" A few weeks ago, I would've done the selfish thing and gone directly for my mother. But after traveling around the country to try and stop Alataris, I realized why I was meant to be a queen. I was put here to think of others, to save the world of Evermore and all who lived there. *What would my mom do?* I stepped in closer to him, so no one would hear me. "No, we free the dragon first. Then look for my mom."

"You sure?"

"It's what she would do." In the pit of my stomach, I knew I was right. What kind of world would she return to if I didn't succeed in freeing Aldesse, the dragon?

"Then let's move."

Tucker and I both turned to look up at the castle that stood in the middle of the island. It was the stuff Disney movies were made of. A winding cobblestone path led up to an imposing white stone castle. The stones were laid so precisely they appeared like smooth white marble with gray veins running through them. A thick oak door stood at the center of the wall. On the corners of the castle were four cylindrical towers with cone-shaped blue roofs on top of each one. A line of windows both on the first and second floors ran across the front of the castle. Small shrubs crept up the walls, covering them in big green leaves and brightly-colored flowers.

This is where he kept me? I couldn't believe it. All that time I'd spent locked up in his dungeon, I never knew I was standing on an oasis of beauty. Even when he took me away from here, I was blinded by the black cloud he'd used to transport us.

Tucker ducked down behind a cluster of bushes big enough to hide an entire house. "Are you ready?"

Was I ready? All this time I'd felt unsure of what my next move was, but standing here now, I knew I was ready to face whatever would come at us. "Yep."

"Stay close." He moved through the thick bushes soundlessly. Each of his footsteps was muffled by the dense foliage covering the ground.

I held my blades at the ready and followed behind him. "How do we find the dragon?"

As if on cue, a deafening roar rocked the tropical forest. Tuck glanced over his shoulder at me. "Follow that."

"It came from that way." I spun on my heels and started in the opposite direction than we'd come from, then smack-dab into a chest the size of a barrel.

I leapt back and held my blades up. The Thrall charged at me with his hands stretched out in front of him. His neon shirt held dirt smudges across it, and his thick black sunglasses had a crack running across one of the lenses. He leapt forward and swung his arms out to wrap them around me.

"Beat it, lurch." I ducked under his hands, then shoved my blade up into his stomach. Black ash rained down on me, falling into my hair. When I stood up straight, I shook it out, letting the ash fall to the ground. My body was knocked sideways, and my back smacked into the ground, knocking the wind out of me. I gasped as another Thrall thrashed on top of me. Not even a second later, the weight was gone.

Tuck wrapped his hand around the Thrall's neck and held him up off the ground. The Thrall kicked his legs out and wrapped his fingers around Tuck's wrist, trying to pry free. Tuck spun his sword, then stabbed it right through the Thrall's chest. More dust fell around me. At this rate, my black leggings and shirt were going to be a light shade of gray. I sat up and rested my arms across my knees.

Tucker stood over me. "You okay?"

I let my blades disappear, then hopped to my feet. "Yeah." I brushed my hands off, then hiked my thumb in the direction of the roar we'd heard only moments ago. "Let's go."

Before I could fully turn away from him, Tuck wrapped his hand around my wrist and pulled me to a stop. "Wait. Before we go any further, there's something I need to tell you."

Now? I looked around, waiting for another thing to jump out at me. "What is it?"

"No, Zin." He let go of my wrist and then wrapped it around the leather cuff on his wrist. "I have to tell you."

My heart leapt up into my throat, and I stared at him with wide eyes. *Is he going to say what I think he is? Here? Now?*

Tucker sighed. "I've wanted to tell you for a while now. But with just the two of us here I don't know what will happen or if we'll survive. So I have to say it now while I can. I'm your sou—"

"Stop." I pressed my finger across his lips. I'd waited so long to figure out who I belonged with. But standing here now, I knew if he told me he was my soul mate I wouldn't be able to concentrate on what we needed to do. If all I saw was him in mind, then we both could die. I had to be on point. We both did. "You tell me after we survive this."

Even with my fingers pressed to his lips, he smiled. His eye bore into mine, and he brushed my hand away.

"Okay, but first." He wrapped his arm around my waist and pressed his mouth to mine.

Heat shot through my body, and I leaned into him, pressing my body up against his. I threw my arms around his neck and pulled him down closer to me. The taste of his minty tongue invaded my mouth. I couldn't fight the sigh that bubbled up from my throat. My nails dug into the skin above his shirt.

Before I was ready to let go, Tucker broke our kiss and stepped back. "Afterward then."

Without another word, he walked past me and into the thick forest.

I CROUCHED DOWN behind a fallen icicle the size of a car. Drops of water ran off the icicle into the puddle my combat boots were sinking down into. Beside me, Tuck lay on his stomach over the ice with his hands cupped around his eyes, looking down into a bowl-shaped arena where the dragon was chained down to the ground. A thick manacle was wrapped around her neck just behind her jaw. Thick silver spikes were on the inside of the collar, stabbing in between her shell-like scales. Streams of blood ran down from each spike. The dark crimson stood out against her white scales.

Tuck pulled the scale from the small of his back and held it out for me to take. "It has to be you who returns it."

"Me? Why me?" I took the scale and slid it into the waistline of the back of my pants. The cool smooth scale felt like an ice pack on my lower back.

"Because I was the one who attacked her." He looked at me over his shoulder.

I crawled up on the icicle next to him and looked out over the bowl where the dragon pulled and thrashed at her bindings. It threw its head back and gave another pained cry. It was surrounded with small cast iron barrels. They were filled to the brim with burning logs, and smoke billowed from each one. The dragon blew a stream of ice down its own back and tail. "What the hell, Tuck? He's burning her to keep her contained?"

The muscle in his jaw ticked. "Cruelty, it's pure cruelty."

I scanned the woods and surrounding area for any sign of life. When I didn't see a soul in sight, I leaned in closer to Tuck and whispered, "Do you think it's a trap?"

"Absolutely." He nodded.

"Then let's see what we can do to piss off Alataris, shall we?" I slid off the icicle and began to tiptoe my way down the big hill leading to where Aldesse was imprisoned. Tucker moved silently beside me like an avenging angel they'd never see coming.

When we reached the edge of the bowl, I stood looking up at the twenty-foot high wall. Without a single word, Tuck swept his hands under my legs and back. I threw my hands around his shoulders to hold on. My pulse quickened in my veins, and I couldn't help but smile. He squatted down and then pushed up, leaping so high my body went weightless in his arms when he came back down to land on the rim of the Aldesse's torture chamber. When Tuck placed me back on my feet, I leaned over the edge.

The walls were covered in a thick layer of ice she must've shot out, but closer to where she was, it was a melted pile of slush. The dragon flipped over onto its back and rubbed its wings in the mucky ice water around its feet. My heart panged for the creature. It needed the colder temperatures to live, and this right here was torture. *What'd she ever do to Alataris to deserve this?*

I sat down on the ledge of the bowl and peeked up at Tuck. "You ever go sleigh riding?"

He shook his head. "I lived in a volcanic valley all my life."

"Then watch this." I pushed off with my legs and threw my hands up, letting my body slide down the ice.

My stomach dropped out from under me, and I wanted to giggle like a little kid, but I kept quiet. The hair blew back from my face, and the cold air prickled my cheeks. The ice soaked through my pants, but I didn't care. My only concern was for Aldesse. The momentum carried me to just outside the circle of burning barrels.

With his fire wings, Tucker floated down beside me, landing gently on his feet. He held his hand out to me. "I'm not sure phoenixes slide."

I placed my hand in his, and he pulled me to my feet. I beamed up at him. "Pity."

Just then, the dragon realized she wasn't alone. She spun around and hissed in our direction. Her lips pulled back from her teeth, and she roared so loudly the ground vibrated beneath my feet.

Tucker summoned his swords to his palms, but didn't ignite them. "I know everyone heard that. We need to hurry up."

I pulled the scale from my waistband and held it high over my head for her to see it. "Shh, we're here to help you." The dragon snapped its mouth closed and tilted its head to the side. I took a step closer. "Remember me? I'm not going to hurt you."

"Zinnia," Tuck warned. "Be careful."

I didn't take my eyes off the dragon. "We're okay,

aren't we, girl? We just need to get this back to you and get out of here."

Tucker stepped up beside me. Her violet eyes narrowed at him, and she hissed. The scales around her neck rose the way a dog's hackles would rise. Her teeth dripped as she bared them at Tuck. When her tail started snapping back and forth, I knew we were in trouble.

I held my hand out. "Tuck, take a step back."

"No. What if you get hurt?" he whispered.

I took another step toward the dragon and held the scale out in front of me. "We don't have a choice." I took another step. The dragon leaned its head all the way down and tucked its wings in close to its body like a lioness about to pounce.

I slid in closer to her, and a growl rumbled deep in her chest, but she didn't move. She lifted her neck just a fraction, so I could walk under her. I took another step under her, and this time, I could see where the scale was missing. It was a single spot in her chest that glowed a bright yellowy orange.

"Zinnia! Look out!" Tuck bellowed a moment before I saw the long sword swinging toward my midsection.

I dove to the side. The blade barely missed my torso as I fell to the ground. The side of my body smacked into the slushy ice. It soaked through my shirt and into the ends of my hair. The scale skittered out of my hands a few feet away. I scrambled on my hands and knees to get to it.

"You think to steal *my* dragon, little girl?" Alataris stood over me with his sword held high over his head. The golden hilt glinted in the fire light. "Think again."

He swung it down, and I held my arm over my body, trying to shy away from the blow. Tucker sprinted toward us, his swords at the ready. At the last second, he dropped to his knees, skidding to my side. He held his swords over my body, blocking Alataris' blow. Metal clanged against metal as Tucker shoved his swords forward, sending Alataris staggering back.

I got to my feet and summoned my duel blades. "I'm not stealing anything. I'm freeing what doesn't belong to you."

Alataris pressed his boney fingers to his chest. His face was all hard angles, but when he smiled, it made him look that much worse. With his gaunt skin pulling tight over his high, sharp cheekbones and his curly black hair falling down the sides of his face in a greasy mess, he looked like a serial killer waiting to happen. In fact, that's exactly what he was, a serial killer. "Nonsense. We all know she belongs to me."

I didn't want to take my eyes off him, not for one second. If I did, he might retrieve the scale from where it lay on the ground. I took a step to the side, blocking his view of it. Tucker moved along with me. We were like two magnets pushing and pulling in unison.

Alataris swung his sword back and forth. "You want her, then you'll have to fight me for her."

This wasn't the time to hesitate or to keep talking to him. I leapt forward, crossing my blades in front of me to block the blow I knew would come. When his long sword connected with the blades, my arms vibrated so hard, I felt the pain all the way down into my shoulders. He threw his weight forward, pressing down on me. I bent my legs, and my muscles quaked with the effort it took to hold him back.

His eyes went full black. "You can't beat me. Just give up."

"Never!" Tucker stepped up beside him and swung both of his swords at Alataris' neck. He ducked under them, and his sword slid back from mine. Alataris swung out and clashed with Tucker. They jabbed at each other so fast their swords and arms blurred into one long motion. I spun on my heels and ran for the scale. A shot of magic smacked into the ground just at my feet, creating a dent, sending dirt and rocks flying up into my face. I leapt over it and pumped my arms harder to get to where the scale lay. Just as I closed in on it, I slid across the ground like I was sliding into home plate at a baseball game. Except this was more important than any game I'd ever played. I wrapped my hand around the scale and scrambled to my feet.

The dragon stomped around nervously, all the while roaring and flailing its long neck at Tucker and Alataris as they battled underneath her. The barbs of her tail went flying right at Tuck's back.

"Tail!" I screamed.

He didn't hesitate. He leapt up into the air and back-flipped right over it.

Alataris too jumped over the swinging tail just in time to follow Tuck. In midair, Tuck shot his wings of fire from his back and held himself high above Alataris. One of his swords vanished, and in its place he held a ball of fire. His face was cold and determined as he launched it right at Alataris.

The evil witch jumped to the side and fired off his own electric energy ball . . . at me.

My hand shot out of its own accord, and I caught the ball. Whenever I'd done this before, I was able to throw the magic back. But this was different. An electric current ran up my arm, and my knees gave out from under me. My body shook like I'd been tasered, yet I refused to drop the scale.

"Zinnia!" Tucker swooped down toward me.

Alataris fired a ball of energy at him just them. Tuck

dove to the side, barely missing the ball. He held himself in midair, trying to get to me but unable to. Alataris threw ball after ball at him. If we were going to win this, I had to get up and get moving. I gritted my teeth and forced my hand to open up and drop the ball to the ground. Sweat covered me from head to toe, and every muscle in my body quaked with pain. I shoved one foot up and then the other. *Run, Zin. Run!* I forced myself to put one foot in front of the other and move toward Aldesse.

Eight witches sprinted in toward me, each of them sliding down the sides of the bowl the way I had. Their long deep purple cloaks billowed out around them as they formed a wall, blocking me from moving. I held my blades up. "Can't you see she has to be free to restore balance to the world?"

A man with black hair that started in a widow's peak and ran down to his hips stepped forward. "High King Alataris is trying to restore balance with the witch court ruling all. Can't you see that?"

I rolled my eyes. "And can't you see that will never work?"

He lifted both of his hands. A ball of magic was centered in each one. "Suit yourself."

"Bring it." I opened my magic and gathered it around me. Silver swirls moved up my legs and down my arms.

I placed one hand over the other with just enough space to hold my own ball of magic within them.

He stepped forward, launching one ball after another at me. I spun to the side, dodging them. I flung my ball of power out at him, hitting him square in the chest. The man flew back ten feet into two of the other witches he had with him. They dropped to the ground in a puddle of limbs. I opened my senses, feeling each one of their powers. They called to me, telling me what each specialty was.

I reached my hand out and siphoned the power from the closest witch. The man dropped to his knees, screaming in agony. The power tasted of icky copper on my tongue and I couldn't get it out of my body fast enough. With my other hand I shot it into a man on the other side of the dragon. Bolts of red lighting ran over his body. He threw his head back and cackled to the sky. When he raised both his arms, he cried out, "For Alataris!"

The red bolts sparked from his palms, but instead of coming at me they backfired right into his own chest. He crumpled to the ground into a steaming pile. I glared at the pile of rubble that used to be the witch. "See, using someone else's power isn't so easy! Is it?"

That's it! I didn't have to fight fire with fire. I could stand back and watch it all burn on its own. I held my arms down at my sides and closed my eyes. In my mind I saw their powers the way I had in my class at the Academy my first day of school. An array of colors, from the brightest yellow to the darkest brown. I flashed my eyes wide-open and couldn't stop the smile from spreading across my lips. I called them all to me. One by one they left the witches and gathered around me, mixing in with my own. The power surged in my body. I felt like my insides would explode if I didn't let it all go.

All at once I let it explode out of me like a bomb, sending all the magic back into a different witch than I'd taken it from. Their screams echoed in my ears as one by one it backfired on them. Behind me swords clashed together again and again. I spun on my heels and summoned my blades back to my hands, ready to take on Alataris.

Tuck and I locked gazes for less than a second. "Go now!"

In that one single moment I knew he saw me, I knew he wanted me to get to the dragon, and I knew he was going to kick Alataris' skinny ass.

I ran under Aldesse. She leapt and jumped from side to side. Her chest was a good fifteen feet off the ground, and there was no way I could do this without her help. "Hey! Hey, you up there. I need your help."

She swung her head all the way under her stomach.

When her violet eyes met mine, her face softened a fraction.

"Listen, girl. I need you to help me, okay?"

She huffed and blew a freezing puff of smoke out at me. I motioned for her to drop down lower. "Just a bit lower so I can put this back on you."

She lowered her chest down to me. I stood under her, looking up into the glowing yellow spot. This close, I could hear the flutter of her heart and feel the old magic running through her veins. This wasn't a creature meant to be captured and broken. She was meant to be free to fly across the sky for an endless amount of days. I placed the scale over her heart and pressed my hand in the middle of it. A bright yellow light erupted from her chest, and the scale morphed in size, becoming a huge half-moon that sat like a necklace around her neck and across her chest. It was gleaming white and shined like the sun.

Aldesse threw her head back and roared with glee. She bucked up on her hind legs and threw her wings out to the sides. Liquid ice seeped from her mouth, and she narrowed her eyes on the chains binding her to the ground. With one deep breath, she shot ice down both of the chains connected to the thick collar around her neck.

I jumped up into the air. "Yes, that's it." I ran over to

one of the chains, then summoned my blades back to my hand and struck it as hard as I could. It shattered into a million pieces and fell to the ground. Aldesse pulled against the other, and it too broke into a rain of metal. She extended her wings and pumped them up, sending intense wind all around the bowl and knocking over the barrels of fire. With her heart scale in place she had the power to get away from Alataris.

I waved my arms. "Go, now. Be free."

She raised herself off the ground a few feet then looked right at me.

"Oh, no."

She extended her large talons out at me and wrapped her claws around my whole body. I slammed my fist on the scales, but it was no use. She tossed me up into the air. My feet went over my head, and I spun around. Before I smacked into the ground, her head shot out and I landed with my legs spread over her neck. *Crap, I'm riding a dragon.* Aldesse pumped her wings, taking me higher and higher. Below Alataris threw his head back and screamed. His face turned a bright shade of red. Before she took me above the clouds, he turned that rage on Tucker.

Dark clouds swallowed us up and I lost sight of Tuck. "No!" I patted the scales on her neck. "No, we can't leave my friend there. We have to go back."

Aldesse hovered in the sky for a moment, shaking her head back and forth. I patted her neck once more. "You don't have to stay, just drop me back down with him."

The dragon surged through the clouds, giving me a full view of Tuck fighting off Alataris. High above them she circled around. Tuck ran at him at full speed. Fire streamed out behind him. At the last second he flipped over Alataris' head and jabbed his sword at him. Alataris spun and countered the swing with his own blade. Tuck leapt back but not far enough. Alataris' blade ran across his side. His shirt tore wide-open and a huge gash marred the side of his rib cage. He pressed his hand over it and stumbled back.

Alataris reached out and wrapped his hand round Tuck's throat then yanked him in closer. Their eyes met and I saw Alataris' lips moving, but I couldn't make out the words. Black smoke drifted from his mouth. Tuck struggled against his hands. Blood poured down his side, soaking his shirt and the ground beneath him. The smoke surrounded Tuck's throat, then drifted into his mouth, nose, and eyes. Tuck threw his head back and his body bowed. His eyes rolled into his head as he inhaled whatever magic Alataris sent toward him. Tuck's body went limp in Alataris' grip.

"No!" I leapt to my feet, trying to balance on

Aldesse's back. I held my hands out, when she began to level out and glided. I pumped my arms and ran down her wing and dove off the side. I held my arms and legs out like I'd seen so many skydivers do before me except I didn't have a parachute. Aldesse roared behind me, but I couldn't think of her. Tuck needed me more than ever now. My mind raced with a spell to make me float down to him, but I just kept plummeting. I couldn't take my eyes off him as Alataris shoved him away. Tuck stumbled back then fell to his knees. He held his hand pressed to his side, looking down at his blood covered fingers. I was so close to him when two large claws wrapped around each of my arms. I looked up to find Aldesse holding on to me. When we got closer, she dropped me down right next to Tuck then took off once again.

I landed in a crouch beside him and grabbed onto his shoulders. "Tuck." I shook him. "Tuck, are you okay?" His head bobbled on his shoulders, but he said nothing.

"Oh, he'll come round . . . sooner or later." Alataris chuckled. "Or not."

I lumbered to my feet and opened my senses, letting my magic gather all around me. Streams of silver circled around me and centered in my palms. "What did you do to him?"

He shrugged. "Zinnia Heart, look at the power you wield."

"Zinnia." My name was a whisper on Tuck's lips. I glanced down at him for less than a second. His eyes were barely open. I knew I had to get him out of here. The color leeched from his skin. His lips turned a pale white.

I held my hands up and faced Alataris. "It is my power and I *will* use it on *you*."

Aldesse dropped down behind me and roared. My hair blew into my face and I couldn't stop the smile from spreading across my lips. "My ride has arrived. We will be going now."

Alataris returned my grin. "Oh my dear, I'll let you go . . . this time. In fact, I couldn't be prouder."

I shoved my hands under Tuck's arms and helped him come to a stand. He moved like a zombie, slow and stiff. I never took my eyes off Alataris. "What are you talking about? I'm doing exactly what I came here to do. I've freed the dragon. The balance will be restored, and you will have failed."

Alataris ran his hand over the tip of his pointy chin. "In a way yes. Your precious balance will be restored. But I will still hold the mother you love and, well, other things. You may have gotten your dragon. But I have more than you can possibly dream."

He took a step toward me, but Aldesse blew a sheet of ice between us. It only stood about four feet tall, but the warning was clear. Alataris held his hands up and took a step back. I climbed up behind Tuck and held on to him. His head rolled around. "Leave now, Zinnia. Leave." His words were so faint.

I wanted to leave, to fly away and vanish from Alataris, but I had to know. "What do you mean?"

"Oh, dearest *daughter*. How magnificent you are."

My breath left me in a rush. *Daughter?* This couldn't be. I opened my mouth to say something else, to deny it all. But the words wouldn't come out. My stomach dropped to my feet and I wanted to vomit. It churned in my belly and I buried my face in between Tuck's shoulder blades. This couldn't be happening. I couldn't be his daughter.

The witch with the long black hair stumbled out next to Alataris. "Sire, don't let them go!"

Alataris held his hand out, stopping him. "I've done what needs doing for now." He folded his hands in from of him. A sinister smile spread across his face. "And we have only just begun."

What does that mean? I wanted to scream out, but the words wouldn't leave my mouth. I could only hold on to Tuck. "Let's go."

Aldesse didn't hesitate to take off. She pulled her

wings in and pumped them hard, shooting us up into the air. I clung to Tuck, but I couldn't take my eyes off Alataris as he faded from view. Though we'd stopped him and freed the dragon, somehow I felt that I'd lost. *Oh yes, we have just begun.*

CHECK out Zinnia and Tuck's biggest struggle yet in *Wicked Hex*. CLICK HERE to order *Wicked Hex*.

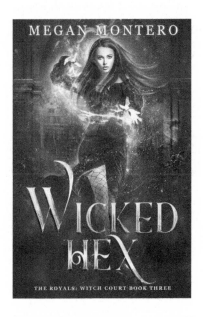

SOME POWERS COME WITH A PRICE...

My life is unrecognizable. I've never been in more danger. I thought I was safe at Evermore Academy. I thought we were finally making progress in this war. I thought I was safe within these walls.

I thought I could always count on Tucker...I thought wrong.

But Now all that's changed. Alataris is coming for me with everything he's got, and no one is safe. He's using the ones I love against me. I'm not sure who is on my side or who has fallen to the enemy's tricks. I want to turn to Tuck, but even he is hiding things from me.

My life is falling to pieces and to fix it I'll have to turn to the one person I know I can't trust...

Click Here to Order *Wicked Hex!*

KEEP the magic alive with *Wicked Potion*! CLICK HERE to order Wicked Potion!

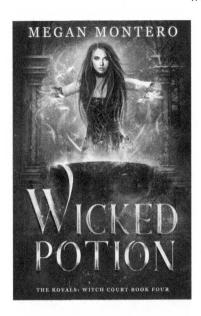

In the war for my power only one will win...

My secrets are starting to surface and in the world of Evermore secrets can get you killed. The sister I never asked for has joined our side. I've hidden the blood tie we share from everyone, including my soulmate Tucker.

I'm hiding too many things from everyone and I'm starting to unravel.

We don't stand a chance against Alataris, not the way we are right now. His power grows every day. There's only one way to beat him – steal his crown. It's the deadliest mission we've taken yet, and it could get us all killed. But without it we've already lost...

See the epic conclusion of Zinnia and Tuck's story in *The Royals: Witch Court Book 5* . To order *Wicked Queen* CLICK HERE!

My power, my reign...

I thought I knew danger, I was wrong. That wicked potion was just the beginning. I feel strong with Tuck by my side, but we're in way over our heads. We need heavenly Fire. It's the only thing that can destroy Alataris' crown. And we can't beat him any other way. That crown is the seat of his power…and I'm going to take it from him.

This is my deadliest mission yet, but I'm out of options and out of time. I have to stop running from him and face my father head on with everything I've got. He thinks he'll win, he thinks I'll buckle after he summons the ultimate evil. But he has no idea what I'd do to protect the people I love. I will take him down, even if I die with him.

This is a family affair and it's time I show my father just how Wicked a Queen can be…

THE MAGIC CONTINUES with *Wicked Omen*! The first book in season two *The Royals: Warlock Court*. To pre-order *Wicked Omen* CLICK HERE.

There's no such thing as magical powers.

Most orphans grow up in foster homes not penthouse suites on the Upper East Side. Everyone always tells me how lucky I am. I know they're right, and I am grateful...but I don't belong here. It all feels so...empty.

In the pit of my stomach I know there has to be more to the world than this. The money, the spoiled rich life doesn't feel like my own. Darkness lingers all around me and I feel it's draw. It sings to me like a siren's song and I've lost the willpower to ignore it.

And then he shows up. His name is Beckett Dust, and he's infuriating. Drop dead gorgeous, but he makes my blood boil. He tells me of a secret world hiding in plain sight, one of magic and power. He paints a pretty picture of a life I'd always dreamed of then takes me to a magical academy to train for a war I have to fight. I'm surrounded by people who want me to fail and he is nowhere to be found.

I'm in over my head and now... they want to use me as a weapon.

FOR THE LATEST NEWS, events and to get free books join my newsletter simply Click Here!

WANT to connect with me and other fans of Evermore? Click Here to join my reader group on Facebook!

DID you read the prequel novella *Wicked Trials?* Do you want to learn how Tucker and his knights got started? Great News- it's FREE- if you sign up for my news-letter! Click Here to sign up and start getting WICKED with your free ebook now!

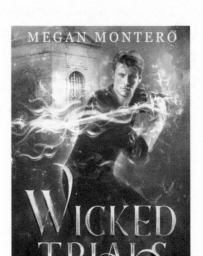

THIS POWER CHOSE *ME*...

Within the supernatural world of Evermore everyone prays their child will be born with the Mark of the Guardian for they have unparalleled strength, intelligence, and *power*...but they have no idea what it's actually like. I didn't wish for this *gift* and I definitely don't want it. I was born a prince, I already had it all. This Mark on my neck stole all of it from me and forced me into a dangerous life I'd gladly trade away if I could...

But now the Witch Queens have ascended and it's time to try and defeat the evil King once and for all. For over a thousand years his cruelty has spared no one as his torturous power grows stronger. He must be stopped now, before his reign destroys everything and anything in his way. So I must push aside my dreams of returning home to the family that cast me out. I must step up and claim the power that chose me. I *must* enter the Trials and become a Knight in the Witch's Court.

There's only one way to prevent the tyrannical king from destroying everything I love...I must become the one thing he can't beat.

WANT to see Zinnia's first days in the wicked world of Evermore. Click here to get your copy of *Wicked Witch.*

It's time to claim my power...

All my life I've lived under lock and key, always following the strict rules my mother set for me. A week before my sixteenth birthday I sneak out of my house and discover *why*. Turns out I am not just a normal teenager. I'm a witch blessed with a gift someone wants to steal from me.

And not just anyone...*the* evil King Alataris.

For a thousand years the people of Evermore have suffered under his tyranny. The Mark on my shoulder says I am the Siphon Witch, one of five Witch Queens fated to come together and finally destroy him. The only thing keeping Evermore safe is the Stone that shields the witch kingdoms from Alataris's magic...and now he's found a way to steal it. Suddenly, I'm sent on a quest to find the ancient spell to protect the Stone. My only hope for surviving is through my strikingly beautiful and immensely powerful Guardian, Tucker. The laws of Evermore state that love between us is strictly forbidden, and it appears I'm the only one willing to give in to the attraction...

When the quest turns more dangerous than expected I realize I have absolutely no idea what I'm doing. I was raised *human*. But I have to learn my magic fast because If King Alataris gets his hands on me he'll steal my magic *and* my life...but if he gets his hands on the stone we *all* die.

THE MAGIC CONTINUES in *Wicked Magic*! CLICK HERE to order *Wicked Magic*.

They all fear my power...they should.

FINDING out I'm a witch was a shock. But now that I'm in the world of Evermore I'll do anything to protect it even if that means dying...

The evil King Alataris has stolen my mother, my life, and now he's taken something that could unleash hell on earth. With a powerful Ice Dragon under his every command there is no telling where he will strike next. The Witch Queens have been tasked with saving Evermore. The only problem? The others fear the wild, powerful nature of my magic and sometimes so do I!

The only one who can help me contain it is my protective Knight, Tucker Brand. But even he has his own set of secrets. My feelings for him are overwhelming and strictly forbidden, if we give into the fire we share for even a moment we will lose everything.

When it comes time to take back what Alataris has stolen we set out on our most perilous mission yet. To save the Dragon and Evermore before it's too late. If we fail, the world as we know it will come to an end…and all will be lost for Evermore.

CLICK HERE To order Wicked Magic!

The Royals: Witch Court Season 1

Wicked Trials- Free when you join my newsletter

Wicked Witch

Wicked Magic

Wicked Hex

Wicked Potion

Wicked Queen

The Royals: Warlock Court Season 2

Wicked Omen- Coming Fall 2019

ABOUT THE AUTHOR

Megan Montero was born and raised as sassy Jersey girl. After devouring series like the Immortals After Dark, the Arcana Chronicles, Harry Potter and Mortal Instruments she decided then and there at she would write her own series. When she's not putting pen to paper you can find her cuddled up under a thick blanket (even in the summer) with a book in her hands. When she's not reading or writing you can find her playing with her dogs, watching movies, listening to music or moving the furniture around her house…again. She loves finding magic in all aspects of her life and that's why she writes Urban Fantasy and Paranormal.

Made in the USA
Las Vegas, NV
03 April 2021